# THE DOOMED PRINCE

## A FEUD SO DARK AND LOVELY 2

LEIGH KELSEY

LYSANDRA GLASS

www.leighkelsey.co.uk

Want an email when new books release - and four freebies?

Join here https://bit.ly/LeighKelseyNL

Or chat with me in my Facebook group: Leigh Kelsey's Paranormal Den

Paperback cover by Creya-tive designs

Ebook cover by Artscandare book design

🌸 Created with Vellum

# THREE FREEBIES FOR YOU

*Join my newsletter for 3 exclusive freebies!*

Fancy some freebies? I'll send you three when you join my newsletter! I promise never to spam you, and I rarely send more frequently than once a fortnight so you won't be overloaded with emails.

Join here: http://bit.ly/LeighKelseyNL

# THE DOOMED PRINCE

## LEIGH KELSEY
## LYSANDRA GLASS

*This book is for everyone who fell in love with Letta and Kier in book one. This book nearly didn't happen, but by sharing, reviewing, and never giving up on the series, you made it possible.*

# BLURB

**For fantasy romance fans obsessed with Sarah J. Maas, Holly Black, and Raven Kennedy. You'll love this snarky, spicy enemies to lovers series.**

I was never supposed to love Kier Kollastus. I was supposed to kill him, return to the human lands, and live happily ever after as a legend.

But fate has a sick sense of humour, and now I'm exiled from the enemy I love, and I have a fracture through my soul because my mate rejected me.

As a human, there's no place for me in the goblin lands, but I can't leave. Tensions are building between Bluescale and Greenheart kingdoms, human rebels have been compelled into murder, and the whole plot hinges on Kier's death.

Everything seems to draw me back to him—the man who cast me out and made absolutely clear he didn't want me.

I already lost my heart, but if I'm not careful, being Kier's wife could forfeit my life.

# 1

This was going to make a compelling chapter in my future bestselling memoir. After I found out my husband was my sister's murderer and *he* found out I'd tried to kill him, I did the only reasonable thing I could. I joined the circus. Well, not the circus, per se—the Troupe of Disaster, whose name spoke for itself. They were actors, and rebels, and little shits. I fit in well. If I ignored the gaping chasm in my chest, anyway.

*I found a way to accept you, to accept that you're my mate.*

*I'm no such thing.*

Fuck Kier, and fuck that. There wasn't a way to undo a soulmate bond. I might not have known much about fate and magic, but I did know that. It was for life, and even hate couldn't undo it.

And I did hate him with all my black, violent heart.

I just hated that he also hated *me*. It was a conundrum.

"Don't trail the point of the sword on the ground, you idiot," I muttered, stretching my legs out on the branch I sat on, watching two troupe members practise sword-fighting. They were hopeless. Honestly, I'd expected better from rebels who constantly provoked the wrath of Bluescale royals and pissed off literally every goblin in the Greenheart realm across the border.

Ryvan, the player I'd met two months ago in Lazankh, turned to give me a sour look. He was just in a pissy mood because he was useless at swordplay and I was exceptional at everything.

He looked different out of costume; instead of being dressed as the king, Kier's father, he wore brown trousers, boots, and a very low-cut white shirt that flashed his chest to anyone who looked at him for longer than a second. Brown hair fell over one eye in a rakish swoop, matching the smirk he wore when he wasn't one second away from throwing a tantrum because he was shit at combat.

"I'd like to see you do better," he purred in a clear challenge.

I raised an eyebrow. The man was delusional.

"No, you wouldn't," Jakoda snapped as she bustled over. The seventy-something woman who kept the troupe organised and on track gave Ryvan a *look*, heavily suggesting he was mad. To be fair, he was. "She'd gut you in an instant."

"You think a *human* can harm a goblin?" Hames— Ryvan's surly opponent—asked with uncalled for scepticism.

The man was a gloomy bastard, and he reminded me of so many dangerous men from Seagrave, but this one was deep, deep blue and came with horns and claws. Same shitty attitude, same tobacco stench following him.

"That human?" Jakoda replied in a biting tone, stabbing her clawed finger through the air at me. "Yes."

I grinned. I had quite the reputation for myself in the troupe after spending eight weeks with them.

"Did you only come here to insult me?" Ryvan huffed, giving the sharp woman a sulky glare.

Jakoda's expression flattened. "I came to tell you to pack your shit up. Zaugustus spotted a hunting party a mile out."

"Another?" Hames demanded, his expression souring even more. "We had to cross the border to avoid one last week."

Ryvan tipped his dark head back to give me a pointed look. I narrowed my eyes in warning, and jumped down to the ground, landing almost silently. Climbing around the rooftops of Seagrave as a teenager converted pretty handily into tree climbing. And since the troupe practically lived in the forest between Bluescale and Greenheart when we weren't performing, there was no end of trees.

Or royal hunting parties, apparently.

Jakoda and Zaugustus—the owners of the troupe—believed the players were being hunted for their treasonous crimes, and I wasn't about to disabuse them of that notion. Ryvan was the only one who knew *Letta* was actually *Zabaletta Kollastus,* princess of the Bluescale Court and wife of Kier Kollastus, the treacherous bastard who killed my sister.

I narrowed my eyes until they were slits; Ryvan rolled his and turned away. He might have known the hunting party was looking for me—the bigger, more desirable traitor than the players—but he would keep my secret. I just wished I knew *why.* I didn't like people having power over me, and Ryvan certainly had power. What was he saving it for? What did he want? Sword-fighting lessons? He certainly needed them.

"Where are we going this time?" I asked, following Ryvan, a scowling Hames as they hurried after Jakoda.

The woman might have been silver-haired, wrinkled, and damn near ancient, but she couldn't half move.

"Verna," she barked without turning. "A shithole halfway out of the forest on the other side."

"Verna?" Ryvan wrinkled his nose. "I've never heard of it."

"It's known for pearlfish," Jakoda replied, stalking through a clearing to where we'd set up a temporary camp. Everything was temporary when you were harbouring a fugitive princess whose sister had killed a Bluescale princess.

I'd had weeks to accept what Natasya did now, but I wasn't sure I forgave her.

I'd spent *years* planning the goblin prince's murder for what he did to my sister, only to find out Natasya killed a kid. She knew what stealing the stone of power would do, and she still did it. I remembered her fervent hatred of goblins, and her reverence when she spoke of our human army and the work she was doing with them, but *fuck*. I didn't know she'd been brainwashed into thinking a child dying was an acceptable loss.

If Danette had been human but still in the way of a victory, would my sister *still* have let her die? Three months ago, I'd have said no fucking way. Even two months ago, I'd have denied it. But now, I wasn't so sure.

I tuned out Jakoda and Ryvan's bickering over deer-skins and headed over to my moth-eaten, shitty tent, knocking out the wooden stakes and poles, and rolling the canvas into my backpack. Everything I owned now was gifted to me by the troupe, not a single thing my own except the clothes I'd fled Lazankh in. And the ring I wore on a chain as if it was a mere trinket and not my wedding ring.

I didn't even have my dagger, and my heart ached fiercely with longing for it. I had blunt knives I could use to defend myself and sharp throwing stars I used in performances, but it wasn't the same.

"Be ready to move in ten!" Zaugustus's loud, booming voice filled the camp. I glanced over my shoulder to watch him prowl around the tents. For such a tall, thin man he was louder than some town criers I'd met.

Zaugustus looked like an emaciated walrus, from his light blue skin and silver hair, to his impressive moustache and tusks. And fun fact: he hated royals. I didn't want to know what he'd think of *me*. I was royal by marriage, but exiled by my sister's murderous actions.

I could have understood Kier exiling me because I tried to kill him. Fair enough, I'd earned that. But he *forgave* me for that.

"Get a grip," I hissed under my breath, and rolled up my blanket, shoving it into my bag and wishing I could bundle my feelings away as easily.

Eight weeks, and Kier exiling me still hurt as much as day one. It gnawed at a place behind my ribs in a constant pain, but I was starting to get used to it. Or at least, getting better at deluding myself that I was used to it.

"Cherish, hurry up!" Zaugustus ordered. "Letta—" He stalked over and cut off when he saw me pull the strings of my pack taut. "Good. Help Aerona get her tent down."

I gave him a dry, snarky look that he pretended not to see, and walked around the dead fire pit to help our youngest member as she struggled with the big pile of canvas and poles. Work never stopped in the troupe; there was either rehearsals, cooking, cleaning, hiking, or scouting to be done.

"I can do it myself," Aerona snapped before I could speak a word. "Back up, Letta. I don't need any help."

I crossed my arms over my chest and smirked down at the teenage girl, not intervening as she battled to separate poles from canvas.

"Sure, you can," I agreed, and couldn't resist reaching down to tug one of her black pigtails.

Looking at Aerona was like looking in a mirror. She was me at fifteen—headstrong, sharp tongued, and street hardened. She was an orphan like me, too, but Aerona didn't have a sister to keep her safe.

"Pull my hair again, and I'll gut you while you sleep," she hissed, yanking on the tent fabric so hard it threatened to rip between her turquoise hands.

She gave me no other choice. I tugged on her cute braid again, and grinned when she hissed deep in her throat.

"If you can sneak up on me while I sleep," I replied lightly, kicking aside a stake that kept her tent secured to the ground, "I'd be impressed."

"And dead," she drawled, now successfully yanking the tent off the ground.

"Mildly injured," I disagreed. "But you're welcome to try. Now roll the tent like this."

"I know how to roll a tent," she huffed with a throaty noise. But she watched my directions and followed them with a scowl.

I left her to it with a smirk, and hefted my own bag onto my back, surveying the troupe around me. They weren't exactly friends, but they were good company, and had become something strangely like family. I'd been lucky to find them, or lucky that Ryvan sensed my magic and knew I'd be a good asset to their cause.

I massaged the forever-aching spot on my ribs as I waited for everyone to finish up. Cherish was trailing behind, as usual.

"Come on, kids," Zaugustus grumbled, his moustache fluttering. "There are hunters on our tail; do you want to be caught and hauled in for treasonous entertainment?"

"I could distract them," Cherish dismissed his worries, fluttering her fingers to demonstrate. A tiny hawk flitted over her head and landed on the old man's shoulder before vanishing. "And I'm done. Happy?"

"Ecstatic," he drawled, shouldering his huge bag.

I didn't wait for his order to roll out; I crossed the camp and headed into the forest, trying to ignore the pain boring deeper through my ribs. Trying to pretend it was heartburn from Jakoda's bland porridge, or maybe a bruise from training with Cherish.

The woman might have been spoiled and prissy with a judgemental side, but she was damn good with magic, and she enjoyed punishing me with gruelling sessions designed to strengthen my power. I'd learned a lot from her, so I endured her attitude even if I wanted to dump poison in her peppermint tea.

"Slow up, Letta," Ryvan called after me, as if *slow up* made any sort of sense.

I turned halfway to give him a warning stare as I walked. I wanted space, not a smirking, annoying bastard trying to sweet talk me into being his best friend forever. It wasn't happening, not today, not ever.

"You know what would lift your mood?" he asked, waggling his eyebrows as he fell into step with me.

"Killing you," I deadpanned, throwing a scowl at the grey-blue sky when a flake of snow swirled down. *Don't you dare snow,* I warned it. The last thing I wanted were boots full of slush.

"So violent," Ryvan teased, his midnight eyes sparkling with mischief. "It's very unbecoming for a princess to be so bloodthirsty."

I slid a knife from my coat and spun towards him in the same movement, whipping it up so fast he didn't stand a chance of avoiding it.

"I'm *no one's* princess," I hissed, tapping his adam's apple with the flat of my knife.

"Letta, stop threatening Ryvan," Jakoda huffed behind us, just out of earshot. "We need him for the show on Wednesday."

"All of him?" I called back, giving the man in question a psycho grin.

"All of him," she confirmed.

"Lucky you," I drawled, removing my knife from my not-quite-friend's throat. "You get to keep all your bits."

Ryvan rolled his eyes, and proved he had a deathwish by elbowing me playfully. "I knew you wouldn't kill me. Admit it, you'd miss me if I was gone."

I slipped my knife back into its hiding place and assessed the trees as we trudged past them, more snowflakes falling. Dammit.

"Sure, I'd miss you," I replied sweetly. "Who else would I use for target practise?"

"Hames," he offered seriously, making me snort.

He had a point; Ryvan might have been an annoying fucker, but Hames was droll and serious and so damn *gloomy.* But he wore a ring of power on every single finger despite never using magic in the eight weeks I'd known him, so I was a *teensy* bit wary of him.

"He wouldn't squeal as much as you, though," I

pointed out—and froze when a distant horn rang through the trees, scattering birds from the canopy. My breath caught in my throat.

Ryvan fell silent, his smirking face uncommonly serious as he spun to give the rest of our troupe a warning look.

Jakoda put a finger to her lips and motioned at the trees. I didn't need telling twice.

I picked my way silently to the nearest tree and climbed as fast as I could, stifling a grunt at the added weight of my pack. Digging my fingernails into the rough bark, I kept an eye on Ryvan and Cherish as they climbed on either side of me. I might have joked about killing Ryvan, but I didn't want anyone to fall and get captured. I was one of them now, and I was grateful to have a place and people who accepted me.

For reasons I didn't want to examine, going home to Seagrave was unbearable. I couldn't return to the barracks where they trained us to kill goblins like Ari, the little kid I'd saved from the Haar. I couldn't go back to Celandrine moulding me into a shining, glorious figurehead to lead a war I no longer believed in.

Who was the bigger monster—Kier for slaughtering my sister, or Natasya for murdering his baby sister in cold blood?

All for war? All for glory?

What good was glory when everyone you were fighting for was dead?

I banished that cheery thought from my head and heaved myself onto a solid branch, stretching out with my back to the trunk for balance. I caught my breath and scanned the trees around me, counting to six—Ryvan,

Hames, Cherish, Jakoda, Aerona, Zaugustus—as everyone settled, safe. Good.

The horn sounded again, *much* closer than before, and a chill went down my back. I controlled my breathing when it threatened to spiral, and forced my thoughts violently away from Lazankh, from Kier, from his best friends who had become almost like friends to me, too.

*Ugh.* I raked a hand over my face, miserably failing at not thinking about them.

My ears pricked at footsteps, and I slammed my hand over the necklace under my coat when it began to glow sapphire in response to my fear. My magic had been stronger lately, and more responsive to my emotions. Luckily, none of the black-clad soldiers who stalked through the trees below bothered to look up, so no one spotted the blue light spilling through my fingers. My heart slammed against my ribs as I watched them pass. There were five of them, the same number as always, and the sight of the familiar uniform made my stomach lurch.

Memories rose: being escorted into the market by them, passing them in the halls of Kier's castle, being surrounded by them after I was presented to the people of Lazankh as Kier's wife and the princess of the Bluescale court.

Pain twisted through my chest, through the bond that tied our souls together, and I gritted my teeth against a hiss.

*I don't miss him. Not for a damn second,* I hissed to myself. *He's a bastard and a nightmare, and what he did to Natasya, the way he brutalised her ... he's a monster. Why would I miss a monster?*

*Because you love him.*

I rolled my eyes at my own inner voice, aware I was losing the last shreds of my sanity by talking to myself.

*Hate is easily mistaken for love.*

*Both can exist in the same heart, and you know it.*

*Heart? What heart? I'm a stone cold, heartless bitch.*

"What is it?" one of the soldiers barked below, snapping me out of my delusional argument.

"A campsite, sir. Recently evacuated."

"Split up," the 'sir' in charge ordered, gravelly and deep. I'd have nightmares about that voice tonight. "Find the tracks."

*You're walking over them, dumbass,* I thought, but kept my mouth mashed shut.

What would they do if they found me? Haul me back to Kier so he could execute me himself? No, that was too out of character for him. That man was too stubborn to change his mind; he'd given his guard orders to kill me, so *they'd* do the job.

This was probably Allenon, the sneering, snivelling bastard who'd stormed the castle, accused Kier of causing the Haar (he was right), and acted like I was good for breeding and nothing else (definitely *not* right.) He was the king's lover, and hated Kier for some mysterious reason. He probably wanted to capture me to use against him.

*Or* Kier's brothers wanted to eat me. Apparently they ate humans.

I shuddered at the thought.

"There's no trail," a woman said minutes later, making the guy in charge sigh.

I exhaled a slow breath of relief and let my head drop back against the tree trunk. We'd evaded this hunting party, but how many more could we avoid?

How long until one of them found me and hauled me to their leader?

I dragged a hand down my face, swiping away a sheen of sweat. It showed the sorry state of things when I'd rather face the human-eating princes than be dragged back to the man who stole my heart and then broke it by exiling me.

# 2

$\mathcal{I}$'d been into Greenheart three times before, and each one had left a very vivid memory. The first time, Aerona nearly got killed by a rampaging beast they called a horse that was definitely *not* a horse. Horses didn't have huge green tusks, teeth as big as my forearm, and *eight* legs. The second time, I ate a delicious stew, found out it was human meat, and then promptly vomited.

The third time, we were smuggling a family across the border and away from the widening spread of white fog. We almost got caught by Greenheart guards who didn't take too kindly to their enemies sneaking into their border towns. Not that the people seemed to mind; it was mostly the royals, and especially their queen, who hated Bluescale goblins.

I stopped trying to understand the politics of it weeks ago.

We hadn't seen the Haar yet, but stories came from every direction and all said the same thing: it was still growing at an alarming rate. Towns had vanished, people had been murdered, and nothing could stop its path.

I massaged the aching knot in my chest and followed Cherish through the doors of an inn. It wasn't the worst place we'd stayed, but the paint was peeling, there was mould on the corners of the ceilings, and the clientele had beer guts and stew in their green beards.

We hadn't seen any Bluescale except us, but I'd braided my hair and wrapped it under a dark purple hat, just in case the royal guards hunting me made it here. A redhead human would stand out pretty obviously among a town full of green-skinned, horned, and tusked goblins.

The violent verdigris of their features took some getting used to; I tried not to gawk at them as Cherish stalked through the taproom and up a step of stairs to the rooms we'd rented. Or rather, the rooms Zaugustus rented for us. I didn't get paid for my part in the Troupe of Disaster, but I got somewhere to stay, food to eat, and for the next five nights, I got a bed.

A bed! It was heaven; I'd never take a mattress and pillows for granted ever again. *Don't think about your bed in the castle, Letta, don't you dare.*

"Do you have to follow so close?" Cherish demanded when we reached the landing, her shockingly beautiful blue face narrowed with irritation.

"Not if you walked faster," I quipped and brushed her shoulder as I passed, my hands full of paper bags brimming with pastry and cream.

"Your ring's glowing," Cherish pointed out, pursing her lips at the telltale circle of blue light on my chest.

"Shit," I hissed, unable to hide it with my hands full.

"You're losing control. Five breathing sets," she ordered, her eyes hardening. "Now."

I grumbled, but followed her bossy command. The last thing I needed was to draw attention to myself when goblins noticed a puny human had magic she shouldn't. I sucked air into my lungs and counted to five, exhaled and counted to five, and repeated it as we tiptoed around a deep emerald woman who'd passed out in the hallway.

Finally we reached the room where our troupe were gathered. I let out my last held breath when Jakoda snatched the bag of cream pastries out of my hand. "Hey! The big one's mine."

"Which one?" She peered into the bag with beady, cunning eyes. "This one?"

*"Yes,* that one," I huffed—and my mouth dropped open when she swiped her wrinkled finger through the cream and smirked before she sucked it clean. "That's it, you're on my to-kill list."

"I wasn't on it before?" She laughed, reaching into the bag and passing me a smaller cream pastry. I scowled, but shoved it eagerly into my mouth. We'd only arrived here an hour ago, and I was starving from the trek through the forest. And I needed a damn drink.

"I'm not staying in this room for three days," Aerona muttered, her arms crossed over her chest as she sat back-to-front on a wooden chair by the little window.

"Yes, you are," Zaugustus argued, unaware there was a smear of cream in his moustache. Ryvan noticed it when I did, and tried to flatten a smile. "We're here to perform for the Greenheart army and scope out a new route for evacuations."

My mood soured at that. If I'd managed to convince the Haar to stop his destruction, we wouldn't need to be here, finding new places to evacuate Bluescale refugees. If things hadn't ended the way they had with Kier, I could have helped him figure out how to stop the Haar. It was part of him—it *was* him. I knew he could stop this, but the Haar had only ever listened to me. And Kier had exiled me.

*Stop thinking about him,* I hissed at myself.

"Letta," Zaugustus said, with the tone of something repeated.

"What?" I muttered, looking up to find I'd stress-eaten my cream pastry. Great. I'd barely even tasted it.

"Daydreaming about a past lover?" Cherish asked, looking down her nose at me as she began brewing tea, not realising quite how close she was to the truth. There'd been no actual *loving* between me and Kier, but damn, there almost had been. I was both glad we'd never taken that final step and furious at myself for missing my only chance.

"Tragically, all my past lovers were murdered," I replied with a faux-sweet smile.

"Because *she* killed them," Aerona muttered, still sulking about not being able to explore a town that had a fifty-fifty chance of killing her.

"Letta, go downstairs with Ryvan and get enough drinks to last us a few hours," Zaugustus cut in, his silver moustache twitching with irritation. He'd wiped the cream out of it while I was zoned out. "We'll pick three potential routes to check tomorrow."

"Why am I your dog's body today?" I complained, throwing the old man a scowl. "I already went out with Cherish."

"I'm hurt you don't want to spend time with me," Ryvan sniffled with a passable attempt at crying. "It really hurts my feelings."

"Aww," I said with zero inflection.

He snorted.

"I need Hames's knowledge of Verna, Cherish's quick thinking—" Well, that was rude. What about *my* quick thinking? "And I don't want Aerona wandering through the town."

"What about Jakoda?" I asked, arms crossed over my chest and my legs throbbing from walking so far today.

"Gout," she replied before Zaugustus could, a smirk on her crafty face. I wasn't sure if the two of them were friends, lovers, spouses, or enemies. They acted like all four interchangeably.

"Fascinating how you scaled that tree with your *gout*," I drawled, but gave Ryvan a long-suffering glance and jerked my chin at the door.

"Yes!" He pumped his fist. "Finally some quality best friend time."

"You are *not* my best friend," I huffed, and threw a look at the rest of the troupe over my shoulder. "If I kill him, that's cool, right?"

"You threaten him so often, it's losing its impact, Letta," Zaugustus remarked, the stern man's eyes almost—almost —gleaming with amusement. "Don't take long."

"I'll be back before you can miss me," Ryvan promised and blew the man a kiss.

I rolled my eyes at his antics and shoved him out the door. No matter what I said, it felt good to have a friend. I missed Calanthe, the best maid in the entire Bluescale kingdom, but at least I wasn't alone.

I tried not to breathe too deeply as we headed back down to the taproom, this time without the scent of vanilla pastry and cream to cover the sweat and stale beer stench. I was used to pubs every bit as classy, but without the nostalgic tang of salt in the air from Seagrave's port, it wasn't the same. It was just gross.

"Where are you going, dickhead?" I called when Ryvan headed left towards a back door instead of into the pub proper.

In answer he waved a polished wooden pipe over his shoulder. I sighed, but followed after him. Ryvan and his damn honey leaf.

I only realised when the door swung shut behind us and he lit a bundle of pale green leaf in his pipe that he'd led me out here to *talk*. I didn't want to talk, but Ryvan was the most stubborn, insistent fucker I'd met since Kier.

*Stop thinking about Kier, for the gods' sakes.*

*"So,"* he said slyly, propping his foot against the brick wall of the pub and casting a look my way. *"Are* you daydreaming about your past lover?"

I bared my teeth on a hiss, sadly pathetic compared to a goblin hiss. "Fuck you."

He shrugged, tipping his tanned face up to the rainy sky. "I'm not questioning your loyalties, Letta. You know I like him more than the rest of that damn family. I wouldn't blame you if you want to go back there instead of trekking around the realm with the troupe. Days like today are no fun."

"I hate it when you're serious," I muttered, tempted to snatch the pipe out of his hand. I settled for shoving my hands in the pockets of my worn leather trousers, scowling down the narrow alley at the back of the pub.

"We're all in the Troupe of Disaster because we have nowhere else to be. But you do."

I laughed, deep and bitterly. "You know *full-well* I've been exiled, Ryvan. Oh, and *the goddamn guards* are looking for me."

Ryvan rolled his arched, blue eyes, exhaling a ring of silver-green smoke. "He's your husband; he can't exile you."

"He can and he has. Nice weather, isn't it? Let's talk about that."

Ryvan raised a dark eyebrow. "It's going to rain, and you miss him."

"I almost killed him," I argued, sucking on a tooth and ignoring the pain twisting through my chest from the bond.

"You're sad as fuck, Letta, and it's hard to watch."

I slid a knife from the concealed pocket in my trousers and spun, pressing it to Ryvan's throat. "Shut the hell up."

"You need to relax a little; try some honey leaf," he said calmly, unfazed by the blade pressed to his gold skin.

I gnashed my teeth and pulled the knife away an inch. Nothing scared Ryvan, and it was starting to annoy me.

"No more Kier talk," I growled.

"Something wrong here, lads?" a deep, unfamiliar voice cut in before Ryvan could reply.

Shit. I dropped the knife and turned, my stomach dropping when I saw three big, beefy goblins with varying shades of green skin, hair, and horns. It was probably shitty that I saw big men and immediately thought they were assholes, but Ryvan straightened and reached for a knife too, so I decided I wasn't so bad.

"Nothing wrong," Ryvan replied smoothly, trying to angle me behind him. I gave him a baffled look at the protectiveness. "Just teaching my friend here some self defence moves."

"She's a girl," the goblin on the left noticed, his greasy stare pouring down my body, a perfect match to his long, greasy hair. Ugh.

"She's a human," the other bookend added, his narrow green eyes filling with a light that made me nauseated. My stomach soured further when the middle, biggest guy fixed his attention on me and licked his lips.

"I'm not food," I warned them, starting to understand why Ryvan angled himself in front of me. "If anyone even *tries* to take a bite out of me, I'll cut you all to bits."

"If we cut *her* to bits," the greasy-haired one murmured, "we can each get a piece."

I sucked in a long breath and smiled when I exhaled. It had been a while since I'd had any excitement, and practising magic with Cherish didn't count.

"Leave this to the professionals, sweetie," I told Ryvan, patting my knife against his shoulder as I strolled past him and grinned at the Greenhearts. "Alright, who's first?"

# 3

*I*'d made a slight miscalculation. I wasn't fighting human assholes, but *goblins* and they were bigger, stronger, and much more brutal. I was faster and smarter, but that wasn't much of an advantage against *three* of them. Even when Ryvan jumped into the fray, we were outmatched.

I really ought to be less cocky. Sometimes I thought the gods heard me boasting and decided to knock me down to size.

"I hate it when food talks," the beefiest goblin remarked to his bookend buddies, earning a loud round of laughter. *So* funny. Give the man a comedy award, seriously.

I raced at him, ducked low, and jammed a knife into his dick, or at least the rough area where it should be. I hadn't technically seen a goblin dick, so I couldn't be sure. I'd certainly felt Kier's, though. And this guy roared so I must have hit the right area.

A meaty fist slammed into my ribs before I could do more damage, and I staggered back with a hiss. That'd be one hell of a bruise; I'd be lucky if I could get comfy enough to sleep tonight. There went my blissful night's sleep in a real bed.

That's what I got for thinking about my husband's cock in the middle of a fight.

"Letta!" Ryvan yelled, knocking me away from the greasy goblin's hand, a ring glowing on the bastard's middle finger as he reached for me. He got a fistful of Ryvan's dagger instead, and wrenched back with a bark of pain as his thumb went flying over his head. Oops. Bye, bye thumb. "Could you stop daydreaming for one damn second?"

I shot my friend a pissy look, but he was right. All thoughts of Kier were banned, from now until forever. Or at least the end of this fight; forever seemed an unrealistic standard to uphold. That treacherous bastard had made a home for himself in my thoughts, and there was no getting him out.

"I think I'll eat those pretty fingers first," the guy with the leering eyes said. "Barbecued in spicy tomato—"

I grabbed my ring in one hand and tore away the control Cherish and I had worked to grow these weeks. My magic had been a raging inferno of pain and fury ever since I left Lazankh. When the numb wore off, I'd been hollowed out and wrath had filled the chasm. It had taken a long, long time to work through the anger, and only finding the troupe had given me some control.

But who needed control when you could rage out of control like a tornado?

Magic blasted from the sapphire ring and out of my palm as I threw it at the gross goblin who wanted to *barbecue my fingers*. It hit him with so much force and power that he lit up from the inside out, his dense skeleton outlined with royal blue magic before his emerald skin blackened and disintegrated.

"What the fuck?" the biggest goblin roared, and the long-haired man's face bleached until he was a sickly green colour.

"That's what you get when you fuck with a human," I said, beckoning them closer with a taunting little crook of my fingers. "Fair warning, I'm spicy enough without a tomato marinade."

"How are you joking about being eaten?" Ryvan groaned, taking a backwards step so unsteadily that I looked at him sharply. Blood trailed down his thigh. Shit. He'd been hurt?

My stomach crashed, guilt swirling through me. If I hadn't been so sensitive to his friendly advice, if I hadn't threatened him with my knife, none of this would have happened.

Then again, he'd dragged us out here to smoke his honey weed, so we were pretty equal.

For a moment, the Greenheart goblins just stared at the spot where their buddy had been, then the big one blurted, "The human killed Arl."

*Arl?* Not Arlo? Arlan? Just Arl? Poor guy.

Well, he'd wanted to roast my fingers and snack on them, so he didn't deserve my pity. Neither did his friends.

I threw my hand up again, tugging on the magic in my ring—and swearing when a sad little trickle rose through my body. No blast of power emerged, no fierce blue jaguar or wicked daggers. Just a little puff of sparks that were extinguished instantly.

"Get back inside," Ryvan hissed, throwing me a tense look.

I got out another knife and nodded, backing up,

keeping an eye on my friend as he moved timidly, pain obvious in his body language.

"This is why humans aren't welcome in Verna," the greasy goblin snarled and launched at us. No, not us, at *me.* Lucky me.

"Because we kick your ass?" I fired back, assessing him for weaknesses, measuring both their movements and strength and throwing together a plan.

"Shit, it's locked," Ryvan growled.

Of course it was. The long-haired goblin wiggled his fingers, green magic playing across his fingertips. The bastard had used magic to lock the door. Typical.

I took a breath, grounding myself, and told myself this was no different than fighting an oversized human. They always underestimated me because I was smaller, and a girl, and not tough-looking like the women who ran in their gangs. But that was my advantage.

"Big talk for something so small," the big, bald goblin laughed.

Case in point. He didn't predict me jumping off the ground, kicking off the side of the pub, and twisting until I landed on his broad back. When my knives drove through his thick green skin into his back, drawing vivid red blood, a howl erupted from him. The vibrations shook my whole body, threatening to unseat me, but I twisted the knives, refusing to be anyone's meal.

A grunt to my left told me Ryvan had thrown himself at the other goblin, so I only had this meathead to contend with. A pang of worry for my friend went through my chest, but the bald goblin threw his head back and slammed it into my nose, and I forgot everything except my own survival.

I'd survived losing my parents and losing Natasya,

survived marrying my goblin enemy, and survived the Haar's vicious fog as it closed around me in Cyana. I could survive this, too. A big, brutish goblin? No problem. I'd already endured Kier, the biggest brute of them all.

*Except he's not,* an annoying voice argued in my head. *He's intelligent and learned and funny.*

I twisted my knives more viciously in the goblin's back, imagining it were Kier's. He deserved it for exiling me, for renouncing me as his wife. After everything *he'd* done, I'd learned to forgive him. To love him. But he couldn't extend me the same damn courtesy?

I cursed when the goblin reached behind himself with big, powerful hands. I evaded one, but the other snared my wrist when I took a beat too long to release my daggers, and I screamed through gritted teeth when he pulled so hard my arm tore out of its socket.

Pain shattered through my sanity.

I abandoned my knives and dropped from his back, trying to use the sudden weight of my drop to detach his grip from my wrist. But it didn't work. His claws dig deeper into my wrist until I couldn't breathe.

Tears burned down my face as he swung me through the air, the pain unbearable, and he tossed me down the alley like I was a pile of trash.

I landed with a scream muffled by my clenched jaw, my vision wavering as pain crested into a brutal storm. I could only make out the rough shape of the goblin. Did he have two heads, or were there two of them?

I panted through my mouth, trying to endure the pain. If I could just get my body to work, I could shove my shoulder back in its socket and get out of here.

"Fuck," I rasped on my fifth blink when I saw there

were definitely two goblins headed my way. What had happened to Ryvan? If they'd killed him...

Rage and power blasted blue light from my ring, but before I could reduce these goblins to ash and bitter memories, something *else* swept in around them and dragged visceral, torturous screams from their throats.

*Get up and run,* I screamed at myself as the temperature of the alley plummeted so fast I shuddered. But the pain throbbing from my shoulder like ripples of an earthquake kept me on the floor, splayed at an awkward angle against the side of the pub.

Cold brick bit into my back and neck, but it was nothing compared to the blistering pain in my shoulder. You'd think as someone who'd had her shoulder dislocated twice before, I could bat this off like it was no problem. In my defence, it was a whole new experience for *this* shoulder. The other one was an old pro. It was also creaky when I drew an arrow or threw a blade.

The blue glow of my ring flickered and died between one surge of pain and the next, but the goblins had gone. Their shadows no longer fell over me. Where were they?

A cold finger brushed a lock of hair out of my face, and I jerked away at the silken touch.

"Touch me and you die," I slurred, blinking my eyes until they focused. But I couldn't see anything through the damn smoke hanging over the alley. Probably the goblin's ashes rising in the wind.

"Safe, Zaba," a soft, husky voice breathed.

"What?" I demanded, my tongue thick and clumsy with pain. I shook my head, but that was a mistake; I jostled my shoulder and pain blared so vividly that I whimpered.

"Safe," that voice—raspy but so damn familiar

—repeated.

Sinking my teeth into my bottom lip when it threatened to cave in, I blinked until the smoke in the air resolved into fog. I could make out the solid white figure leaning over me, built as powerfully as Kier, the features of his face the same as my husband's but made of opaque mist instead of rich bronze skin.

*Or deep, vicious blue,* I reminded myself, stuck on the memory of Kier transforming in front of me, terrifying teeth bared as he exiled me.

"Zaba," the Haar murmured, stroking a knuckle down my face.

"Kier," I slurred. "What are you ... doing here...?"

The Haar's cool fingers caressed down my jaw, and I was in no position to stop his exploratory touch. It felt so good to be touched again, to be—to be back with him. At least the Haar didn't hate me, even if the rest of Kier did.

"Sorry I—shot you," I panted, my vision hazing with pain again. "Didn't know it would—hurt you."

"Hurt," he echoed, his brow knotting. I laughed deliriously. He was made of magic, grief, and mist—how could his brow knot? "Zaba, hurt?"

"Mm," I confirmed. "Need to push my shoulder back in."

He blinked at me, milky eyes wide with pain. Had he had eyes before? I couldn't remember. His touch drifted down my neck, tender enough that it made my whole heart hurt. It took me a moment to realise the throbbing pain in my chest where the mate bond lay broken had stopped aching. It was soothed by the Haar's presence.

"Zaba—" he began, but his fingers brushed over my injured shoulder, and the pain was so brutal and sudden that I blacked out before I heard the rest of what he said.

# 4

*I* knew I was dreaming, but I defiantly ignored that fact, stretching out in the plush cushions of my bed in the Lazankh palace. Fuck, it felt good to be home. Familiar scents surrounded me, hyacinth and sweet, earthy spices wrapping around my senses like a caress, the silk of sheets on my body so far beyond heavenly that I groaned.

"Keep making noises like that, and we'll never get out of bed," a dry voice remarked.

I cracked an eye open, and was treated to the sight of Kier splayed across the bed beside me with the sheets slung low around his waist and his muscular chest bare. Glorious golden skin tempted me to touch.

"Don't make promises you can't keep, husband," I replied, rolling onto my side and gliding a hand over his heated skin, fingers tracing the contours of his stomach.

Calloused fingers stroked over my wrist, deceptively soft but vicious a moment later. I inhaled a sharp breath when he rolled on top of me, pressing me into the mattress with the full weight of his body and trapping my wrists above my head.

My heart raced, adrenaline and desire roaring through my blood. The sheets tangled between us.

"Oh, I keep my promises, Zaba," he purred, his thighs tightening around mine, keeping me trapped as he dipped his head to run a trail of open-mouthed kisses down the sensitive line of my throat. "I'll keep them so well you'll forget your own name."

In hindsight, I shouldn't have scoffed. But there was something about Kier's unending cockiness that pushed all my buttons.

I was unprepared for cruel fingers to find my nipple through my loose cotton sleep shirt and pinch. Hard.

I gasped, bucking up off the mattress, and Kier laughed against my neck, grazing his teeth to send a violent shiver through me.

I crept my hand under the pillow, letting out a deep moan to distract Kier—and because he now stroked a circle around my nipple to soothe the sting. The second cold steel met my fingers, I brought the dagger around in an arc and pressed it to Kier's throat, pushing an inch of distance between us.

The bulge against my hip became as hard as iron when the sharp edge met Kier's skin, and he groaned.

"Bleed me if you must, but I need to be inside you," he said huskily, tilting his head to press the knife deeper.

I hissed and relaxed my pressure. I wasn't trying to actually kill him.

"You're unhinged," I told him. "Are you trying to die?"

He didn't answer. His hand made a slow, exploratory path up my chest to my neck before finally caressing my jaw and bringing me in for a kiss. I shoved my knife back under the pillow so I could sink my fingers into his long, dark hair, holding Kier to me as he nipped my bottom lip and kissed me so fiercely that my head spun.

The sweet musk taste of him exploded across my tongue, filling every sense until I was drowning in him but desperate for more. His hair hung around us, brushing my neck like silk, making me shudder as he trapped my bottom lip between his teeth and threatened to bite.

*Do it,* I taunted him silently, holding his midnight blue eyes. He was so close I could make out the flecks of silver among the blue, the tiny scar on his stubbled cheek in sharp detail.

His chest vibrated against mine with a growl, and sharp fangs nipped my lip, filling our kiss with the taste of copper. His lips and tongue met mine roughly, feral with need when I gasped at the scratch of pain in my lip. It stung like a bitch, but it seemed to echo the pulse of intent need between my legs.

"I'll never get the taste of you off my tongue now," Kier groaned while we gasped for breath, his eyes almost black as he tore the covers away and knocked my thighs apart. My shirt had ridden up and Kier had shucked off his clothes some time during the night, so my bare skin brushed his as he settled between my legs, grinding his hips into mine. "You're seared into my senses, wife."

Why did it get me so hot when he called me wife in that tone? I tightened my fingers in his hair and dragged him back for more kisses, my lips urgent and demanding as his hands wandered down my shirt and found the hem. Anticipation made my body tingle, inner muscles clenching with impatience as Kier's fingers stroked my hip bone and ventured lower, but not nearly low enough.

He broke our rough kiss with a growl, his lips

fastening to my throat and hot, panting breaths grazing my skin.

"Is there something you want, Zaba?" he teased when I bucked my hips, trying to move his hand where I needed it. His gentle stroking was *maddening,* so damn close that my clit throbbed wildly.

"You know what I want, bastard," I snarled, tugging on the roots of his hair and earning a deep, vicious rumble. My toes curled. Violent pleasure hung in the air, so close I could touch it, and I panted for breath.

His teeth scraped my throat, a hand roughly pawing my breast and tugging my nipple. Sharp pleasure shot directly to my pussy, making me drip.

"Badly behaved girls don't get what they want," he warned.

"Badly behaved girls will *take* what they want if you keep teasing them."

"I'd like to see you try, mate."

My eyes rolled back a little. If *wife* made me weak, *mate* ruined me.

I released my grip on Kier's hair, roughly pushing his hand lower. He glided through my wetness, the pad of a finger rolling over my clit, and I sank my teeth into my bloody lip and moaned.

"Are you trying to earn a punishment, Zaba?" he asked, a dark tone to his voice that made me even needier. "Fuck, you're soaked for me."

*"Kier,"* I complained when he grabbed my hand and pressed it flat to the bed, his other fingers still on my hot, needy pussy. "Don't tease."

A dangerous smirk curved his bearded face as he peered down at me, flushed and panting under him. "But you're so beautifully responsive when I tease you."

I bit my tongue when his fingertips glided around my clit, never touching, driving me wild with impatient need. On his third teasing circle, the whine slipped off my tongue and Kier rewarded me with a kiss. His smirk imprinted on my lips, and my heart pounding faster.

"Say please," he ordered, edging even closer to my clit but refusing to touch my swollen bundle of nerves.

"Kier," I hissed, digging my fingernails into his hips so hard I left marks behind. "Stop fucking about. I need to come."

Dark eyes flashed, and fingers wrapped around my throat, pressing my head back into the pillow. It didn't hurt, but the idea that he *could* hurt me, that he had total power over me, made my body scorching hot. I bit my lip against a whine.

He leaned over me and met my eyes with ruthless steel. "Say. Please."

My breath caught in my throat. "Please."

"Good." He ruined me with a tender kiss to my brow.

I'd barely processed my tremulous emotions when his fingers found my clit with unerring intent and my hips bucked off the bed.

"Fuck," I moaned, grabbing his arm as he lavished my neglected clit with fierce attention. A deep sound of satisfaction rumbled in his throat at my response. "Harder, Kier."

He applied more pressure, and my head fell back into the pillow, teeth sinking into my bottom lip.

"I want to taste your climax," he said in a deep, throaty voice. That was all the warning he gave before he crawled down my body, his tongue trailing a greedy, sucking path that made my inner muscles clench hard.

Firm hands pushed my thighs wider so his broad

shoulders could fit between them, and his tongue glided over my hot, sensitive flesh. Tingles rose wherever his mouth met my skin, his fingers keeping their perfect pace on my clit and his hair brushing the delicate skin of my inner thighs, making me shivery and hot.

"Kier, *fuck,*" I gasped when he adjusted the angle of his fingers on my clit and pure sensation shot through me. He lapped at my entrance when I dripped hot arousal.

Another bright crash of pleasure made me whine. My hand shot down and I coiled my fingers in his hair, gripping hard as he exploited that new angle and made my mouth hang open, my body tensing as pleasure coiled in my stomach.

Holy fuck. Holy fucking gods.

"That's it," he groaned against me. "Come all over my tongue, mate."

With those words, my hips bucked into him and the coiling heat broke in my lower belly.

I came so hard I saw stars.

My legs ended up wrapped around his head as Kier feasted on me, a long, steady growl vibrating against me as he lapped up every drop, sending my climax into a higher sphere. I pulled his hair, choking on air as waves of pleasure hit me with destructive power.

When the last wave shuddered from my body, my legs fell to the bed and left me limp and languid. *Ruthless gods...*

Kier wore a wicked, smug grin as he slid up my body, kissing every place he passed, spreading warmth and contentment through my soul. I waited for his lips to brush mine, for his arms to wrap around me, but instead a rough hand grabbed my shoulder and—

Pain stabbed my eyes.

Awareness came sluggishly, and so did the rough bricks pressing into my back, and the dull ache throbbing in my shoulder.

My body thrummed with pleasure and I was *soaked* between my legs, but all at once I realised I wasn't spread across a luxurious bed. I was sprawled on the floor of a cold alleyway, and instead of Kier crawling up my body for another scorching kiss, it was Ryvan's frowning face that filled my vision.

"Ugh," I groaned, and closed my eyes again.

I wanted my damn dream back.

# 5

*I* should have enjoyed my part in the Troupe of Disaster's play far less than I did. Especially considering a good chunk of the Greenheart goblin army had crammed into the coliseum to watch us. Word had gotten out that the troupe were touring around the Bluescale kingdom mocking their royals, so naturally their enemies wanted to see the show.

This time, Hames was dressed in bright finery and supposed to be Kier. I'd offered him some constructive criticism when he played my husband like a saviour on a shining charger during rehearsal. *Less smiling, more scowling, and honestly ditch the bright colours for funeral black.* He'd ignored me, which was usual for Hames.

Zaugustus stood to one side of the stage, watching the Haar—better known as Ryvan doused in white paint and a bed sheet—flounce around in an acrobatic routine more reminiscent of a poodle having a mad half hour than the fog destroying our towns. The king did nothing to intervene, exactly like when I watched this show in Lazankh.

Only here, the goblins chuckled and guffawed when he continued to stand still like a lemming.

My big performance was in the second half, and I was looking forward to it immeasurably. I didn't think about the embarrassingly hot sex dream I'd had of Kier as I watched Hames fight the Haar in the play. I didn't think about the Haar's soft, husky voice as he killed the goblins who threatened to eat me. *Safe, Zaba.*

I was alive instead of goblin food because of him. Because a part of Kier still cared about me, and wanted me alive. I didn't know what to feel about that.

I was glad when intermission came, and the area behind the heavy green curtain became a whirlwind of activity. Cherish shoved through the chaos and glided onto the stage, her beauty hushing the crowd and the violin in her hand piquing curiosity. Bright, joyous notes of music filled the coliseum as she began to play, keeping the troops entertained while we got ready for the second act.

Jakoda thrust new costumes at everyone—except me and Aerona, who were ready to go in our ridiculously poofy dresses. I almost missed the delicate seafoam lace of my wedding dress, with its beautiful flowers pressed between layers of tulle. This thing was a crinoline monstrosity.

"Why does Hames get to wear leathers?" Aerona demanded, picking at the pink fabric of her dress. They looked ridiculous on both of us, but paired with her scowling blue face, it was extra comical. That was the whole point.

"Letta, you're on," Zaugustus barked when Cherish's violin piece finished on a hopeful flurry of notes. The old man hurried over with his cheeks tinged purple by stress, the rest of him flushed too. "Make your eyes wider than last time. I want you to look completely oblivious and baffled."

I gave the man a double thumbs up. "You got it, boss."

"She's going to do something over the top," Ryvan warned him, trying his best to scrub the white paint off his hands. It wasn't working.

"Don't," Zaugustus growled, his moustache ruffling, somewhat undercutting the warning look he gave me.

"Do?" I pretended to mishear, heading for the green curtain. "Okay! I can do that!"

"Letta," he rumbled, grabbing me before I could escape. His clawed blue hands were strong but gentle as he held me in place for a long stare. "Be careful. Don't get too close to the audience. Don't let anyone know you're human; Greenheart aren't as accepting as Bluescale goblins."

"I know," I replied, my stomach rippling with sudden nerves. "But I'm more dangerous than your average human; I'll be fine. Don't worry, old man."

His lips pressed thin under his moustache. "You're troupe; I worry about all of you."

My heart warmed at the acceptance, emotion weakening my soft heart for a moment. But I hid it behind a wide grin. "Knew you liked me, old man."

"Go," he barked gruffly, releasing me to give me a nudge towards the stage as Cherish ducked backstage, her eyes bright and chest heaving. "And remember what I said."

"Be careful; I know."

Zaugustus gave me a long look that told me he knew I

*wouldn't* be careful, but he didn't stop me ducking out through the gap in the green curtain. Cherish gave me a smug look at the hushed quality of the crowd, her nose high in the air.

I rolled my eyes. Yes, she was amazing, yes she was stunning enough to hush even the roughest people, yes she was an actual angel walking the mortal realms to bless us with her presence. But could she throw a knife and pin someone to a wardrobe by their jacket *without* nicking their skin? *I* could, and I had yesterday when Ryvan kept pushing for answers about our miraculous survival.

No one knew the Haar had saved us; Ryvan had been passed out and no way was I telling a soul.

Eyes fixed on me and my absurd lilac dress as I flounced across the stage in a huff and flopped dramatically onto the elegant sofa Jakoda wheeled out during the intermission.

"Just *where* is my husband, the Bluescale king?" I lamented, loud enough for the crowd to hear.

Someone snorted.

Another yelled, "Probably screwing his advisor. I can show you a better time, sweetheart."

Better than the king? Probably. Better than the sex dream I'd had of Kier? No fucking chance.

I let out a loud sigh and flung the back of my hand to my forehead. "If he doesn't come home soon, I'll die of heartbreak."

I peered out from my fingers, scanning the crowd full of bulky green men and women, my eyes snagging on the big, green crystal guns some of them held. A memory rose of climbing Kier's castle with a modified version of those guns. I shook it off when Aerona came through the curtains in a tantrum.

"Mama, the courtiers are saying bad things about Daddy again," she whined, really putting the full weight of her bratty attitude into it.

I rose in a rush. "But what could they possibly say? The king is the greatest, kindest, bravest, most handsome person in the world."

The crowd laughed, yelling their disagreements. I felt a teensy bit bad about making fun of Kier's parents, but his dad sounded like a real dick, and he hadn't even mentioned his mum, so I tried not to feel so bad. Plus, he'd *exiled* me so they were my enemies.

Aerona huffed, her hands on the hips of her big, meringue-esque skirt. With her hair in pigtails and rouge on her cheeks, she looked every inch the petulant princess. "They say he's a lousy king, and instead of fighting the war he sits at home staring into the mirror, like a budgerigar mesmerised by his reflection."

I faked a horrified gasp.

The crowd guffawed, unsettling their massive weapons with their laughter. The guns were huge, three times the size of the ones Xiona made. Why did they need so many guns? Why bring them to a performance when there were no humans nearby to fight? Well, except me, but as far as anyone knew I was a small goblin in mortal disguise.

"They say he's a bad father," Aerona went on, stalking across the stage. The Greenheart goblins *loved* all the insults to the king, getting rowdier with every word. "And a fool. They say he couldn't even win a fight with a human."

"Or a goblin," a coarse voice called from near the back, earning a fresh round of chuckling.

*Or a goblin.* The words repeated in my head even as I

faked an outraged cry. "Such *awful* things. How will we survive the indignity?"

At that moment, Zaugustus strutted onto stage like a peacock, dressed in finery (ish) and dazzling jewels (fake.) His hair had been dusted with white, striking against his deep blue skin, and gold was wrapped around his horns and long fangs.

"Behold!" he yelled with impressive volume. "The most glorious king in all the realms. Gaze upon my magnificence!"

I jumped to my feet and spun, clasping my hands to my chest, but I watched the crowd from the corner of my eye. Something was up with this army, and I had no idea what we were doing here, in another realm, mocking the Bluescale king. Couldn't they put on their own show?

Why invite a travelling troupe? Why bring *guns?*

The crowd leaned forward and booed at the sight of the king, and a couple produced tomatoes and rotten fruit from gods knew where. I legitimately didn't want to know *where* they'd had them stashed.

The audience guffawed as a rotten fruit burst over Zaugustus's bright cloak. I exchanged a glance with Aerona. This was getting ugly fast.

Even if the soldiers were loving the show, the energy was so high and charged, it made my skin buzz.

"Bluescale bastard!" a deep voice boomed.

Worse, more vulgar insults followed, but Zaugustus took it in stride and bowed. I respected him so damn much in that moment.

"My treasured subjects, I've come to grace you with my presence." Like he was the people's king, he began blowing kisses, acting completely oblivious to the hatred.

To be fair, from the accounts I'd heard, the actual king was every bit as blind.

A tomato nailed Zaugustus right in the cheek. Oof. Seeds and tomato guts covered his face.

Ryvan strode onto the stage at just the right time to distract another soldier hurling rotten fruit at Zaugustus. I caught a glimpse of him and stifled a laugh at the stiff way he walked, his nose stuck in the air. When he spoke, his voice was nasally and smug. Spot on for Allenon. It was uncanny.

*"Sire,"* he simpered. "I need a moment of your time."

"And your cock!" a Greenheart goblin boomed, to uproarious laughter. Ah, men. The same in any species.

What followed was a messy blend of scripted tomfoolery, improvised mockery, and audience-fuelled ridicule. Poor Zaugustus was covered in rotten food, and I had a nasty wet spot on the back of my poofy dress. I'd staggered dramatically when it hit me and pretended to almost pass out from the abuse. Someone had offered to improve my mood with their giant cock, which I didn't consider helpful.

Whoever had booked the troupe for this show would have been better off reserving a brothel for this lot. If they weren't insulting the king's manhood, they were boasting about their own. They were obsessed.

We ended the show with a satirical song and dance number about the king's cowardly flight while his citizens faced the Haar. I put my whole heart—and my whole chest—into the routine.

I had to heave the bodice of my dress up halfway through as it threatened to fall down—some of the stitching had come undone, probably thanks to the added weight of rotten peaches. Relieved it was over, I belted out the final line.

*"King Roscoe, that treacherous prick!"*

Someone in the audience added, "King Roscoe has a tiny dick," with perfect timing and rhyme.

Like I was saying. Obsessed.

I broke character to laugh, so damn glad the show was over and we could get the hell out of this place. No one had thrown fists; no blood had been drawn. We'd been lucky to get through it.

Movement drew my eye to the back of the coliseum as people began to leave their seats. No, these people were coming *in.*

"I'm afraid you missed the show, gents," Ryvan called, still using the snooty voice he adopted to impersonate Allenon. I snorted.

"I don't think we have," the smallest newcomer called back. Actually, they were all pretty small for goblins. Even in their human forms, they tended to be taller, broader, and just overall more intimidating. There were three men around my height, and one maybe six foot two.

The one who'd spoken took something from his pocket, too small to see from the stage.

"What's going on?" I asked Aerona.

"How the hell should I know?" she snapped, her brows low over her eyes.

Ryvan crossed the stage, his expression dark as he came to stand between me and Aerona.

I only realised what the man had taken from his pocket when he struck it against rough card. A match.

"What are you gonna do?" a big, green, horned woman taunted. "Light a candle?"

"Actually," he replied with pure, seething hate in his voice, "I'm going to light up every goblin scum in this place."

Ryvan and I grabbed Aerona at the same time, pushing her behind us. I realised far too late why the newcomers seemed small for goblins. *Goblin scum.* They weren't goblins at all; they were human.

We spun towards the curtain and the safety of backstage, but a terrifying *whoosh* exploded through the coliseum, and fire encircled the stage and seating. It was hot enough to make my skin prickle, and so sudden that I flinched.

The humans hadn't brought a single matchbook; they'd planned this meticulously. They must have rigged the place before we got here, and used something scentless. I hadn't smelled alcohol or gunpowder. None of us had.

"Go!" I yelled, pushing Aerona and Ryvan towards a spot near the curtains that hadn't caught fire yet, and turning to search the stage for the old man. "Zaugustus!"

"Coming," he yelled from the other end of the stage. "I'm right behind you."

Of all the ways I thought I'd die, perishing in a blaze set by my own species was not it.

"I'm not dying today," I growled under my breath, jumping in surprise when my ring flared with bright blue power.

"None of us are," Ryvan snapped, his hand wrapped around Aerona's upper arm as we ducked under the curtain, narrowly avoiding a scalding flood of fire. Gods, I'd never realised how *loud* fire was, how it flickered as loudly as a thunderstorm.

Heat grazed the back of my neck as we moved through the backstage area, and I spun with a panicked gasp, making sure my ridiculous dress hadn't caught fire. Through a gap in the curtain, I saw Zaugustus hurrying after us, and goblins surrounding the humans like a mob. But deep growls of pain told me the humans were putting up a good fight. What the hell was happening here? Since when did humans sneak into goblin lands and attack them?

But hadn't Natasya done the same?

Were these the rebels who stole Kier's gemstone and killed Danette? Were these the bastards responsible for my sister's treachery—and her murder? If she hadn't fallen in with them, she'd still be alive.

I was too furious with my sister right now to tell if I still hated Kier for what he did. I'd have done the same as him, I knew that without a doubt. But there was no confusion at all marring my hatred for Natasya's rebel friends. I wanted them all dead.

"Faster!" Ryvan barked as fire crawled up the green curtain and caught on the ropes rigging up sets. Smoke unfurled through the backstage area, catching the back of my throat and making me cough.

"Out here," a familiar and welcome voice shouted at the far end of the space. Cherish.

We followed her voice past a stack of wooden backgrounds, the fire hunting us faster than I thought possible, hungrily devouring timber and velvet. Behind us, growls and cries came from the coliseum, a chorus of pain that chilled my blood.

Had Natasya done things like this before she was killed? I knew war was messy and heartless, and it killed anyone in its path. But *this*? A calculated attack on a *theatre* of all places? Sure, the theatre was full of soldiers, but the humans out there didn't care whether the troupe lived or died, and *that* was the part that wound me up.

I might have been a thief and assassin, but the people I killed deserved to die. Cherish? Aerona? Ryvan? No fucking way. Not even Hames, the grumpy bastard.

"Come on," the grump himself barked when we neared the door. He waved his hand to usher us faster, as if we weren't running at full speed. Worry tightened his rugged face; he scanned us for injuries with intense dark eyes.

I turned to make sure Zaugustus wasn't falling behind and—*where was he?*

"Hey, old man?" I yelled. "Where are you?"

Ryvan paused at my question, but he pushed Aerona onward. Hames grabbed her and hauled her out the door, wrestling her to safety even as she struggled and almost tripped over her pink skirt.

*"Zaugustus!"* I screamed, scanning the insatiable flames destroying backstage, the green curtain now in tatters around the stage.

"Where the hell *is* he?" Ryvan demanded, following me closely as I took a tentative step, avoiding the worst of the fire. I only managed to take three steps before a violent crack tore through the timber above us, and my breath caught on a shriek as it snapped. Ryvan grabbed me and heaved me aside, the two of us stumbling out of its path and *narrowly* avoiding being set alight.

Shaking, I stared at the burning space, the hours of work in set design turning to cinders. My gaze snagged on a colourful shape on the floor being eaten at by merciless flames. No. *No.*

Ryvan dug his fingers deeper into my arms when I

tried to twist away, to run to the old man. My heart raced and crashed at the same time, a brittle shakiness starting in my stomach. *No.*

"Let go of me!" I snarled, struggling against Ryvan, panic clawing up my throat as flames devoured Zaugustus's jewelled costume—and him within it. "Ryvan, he's *there*—"

"He's gone," he disagreed, his voice a guttered, empty thing. "He's gone, Letta."

I shook my head fast, rage and denial making my heart frantically fast. I shook all over, each breath a shattered gasp. I couldn't take my eyes off Zaugustus's body.

Ryvan didn't know he was dead, he could still be saved.

My jaguar burst from me in answer to my desperate hope, filling the inferno with cerulean light. While I trembled on the edge of shattering completely, she leapt, unhurt, over burning wood and collapsing beams until she reached Zaugustus. My friend. The man who'd taken me into his troupe when I had nowhere else to go.

"Shit," Ryvan breathed, his arms tightening around me, both of us watching my jaguar reach the burning body. Hope choked off my air, or maybe that was the smoke. I shook as I waited, watching my jaguar push her nose against Zaugustus's neck, uncaring of the fire that consumed him.

*Save him, get him out of here,* I ordered her.

But she sat back on her haunches and gave me a slow, sad look amid the flames, and I knew.

Zaugustus was—he was—

A roar ripped from my throat, human and pathetic but full of fury and—and grief. I hadn't felt this way since Kier exiled me.

When my voice gave out and weakness took hold of me, I felt empty. I let Ryvan drag me through thunderous flames towards the exit as the coliseum's theatre came crashing down around us.

Zaugustus was dead.

# 6

The numbness lasted three hours. I'd barely eaten the stew Hames brought up from the pub downstairs, and not just because the meat was questionable. I had no appetite. I couldn't stop seeing Zaugustus's body on fire. We couldn't save him, but we shouldn't have left him there.

Humans did that to him. My own damn people.

I could have been the one burning, and I'd have been acceptable collateral for them.

I rolled over on the luxurious mattress I no longer gave a shit about, listening for a change in Aerona's and Cherish's breathing. They were sound asleep. I should hope so with the amount of sleeproot I dumped in the beer we all shared earlier. We might not have felt like eating, but we sure felt like getting pissed, so it was easy enough to knock everyone out. I'd been careful not to have too much, so I was still awake.

If anyone knew what I was planning, they'd talk me out of it. Besides, the troupe needed to sleep; I couldn't imagine everyone getting a lot of rest in the next few weeks. Hell, the next months.

"Ruthless gods," I hissed when the door creaked under my hand, but my friends kept sleeping. As I passed, I checked in on the guys—fast asleep—and peered in on Jakoda in the room she'd shared with Zaugustus. She'd passed out sitting up. My heart squeezed tight.

Months ago, I'd never have believed I'd be genuine friends with goblins, that I'd feel like total shit to lose one of them. I was starting to think I'd had no sense of real empathy in Seagrave. I'd only cared about myself and Natasya. I was learning more about myself the longer I spent in the goblin lands. A difficult lesson was that caring about people only got you hurt.

I checked my knives and my ring were in place as I jogged down the stairs and through the pub, feeling for the place inside myself where magic had been growing steadily stronger every day. When I first used magic in Cyana, there was no way I could have held onto it this long.

In the chaos after the fire, fleeing through the city, all of us ruined by grief, no one had noticed that my jaguar wasn't by my side. Ryvan hadn't noticed her staying in the theatre, prowling through the coliseum to find the humans' trail.

*Show me,* I ordered my magic now. After an embarrassingly long stare from Cherish last month, I'd learned I could think commands instead of saying them out loud. Anything that didn't make me sound like a lunatic talking to herself was a win.

The dark stone buildings around me fell away, replaced by a huge viaduct formed of green stone blocks. The river that snaked around the coliseum flowed all the way to the massive stone arches. My jaguar treaded water in the dark water; the bastards must have fled down the river, but she followed. I'd decided she was a she.

"Got you," I hissed to the bastards who didn't know their breaths were numbered, a feral grin curving my lips.

They were going to die. Painfully.

It took me the better part of an hour to cross the town, ducking into shadows whenever a goblin passed. I was *not* interested in another matched set of brutes thinking I'd make a tasty meal.

*Stay close,* I told my jaguar as the viaduct came into view. It was impressive as hell, and even more so when I saw the pearlfish Jakoda had mentioned leaping from the still waters at its base.

"Fancy," I murmured, assessing the rows of tight, narrow houses that lined the roads around the viaduct. Fishermen's homes, most likely. As I crept down the steep path, the nets and boxes outside confirmed it. What were human rebels doing among goblin fishermen?

My jaguar slunk out of the water, bright glowing blue against the dark of the night, her teeth bared like she was already thinking about ripping people apart.

*Can't you dim your brightness?* I muttered. *They'll spot us coming a mile off.*

Her turquoise glow softened to a midnight blue as she stalked up to a house with a lacquered black door weathered by salt. My grin returned. Perfect.

*Creep around the back,* I told her as I approached the front. *Don't let them escape.*

She dipped her dark snout and trotted eagerly around the row of narrow houses. I shook my head, watching her. It was surreal having magic at all, let alone a jaguar that had her own personality, loved to hunt, and hated Hames. I didn't know why she disliked this big guy —he was grumpy but harmless—but she snarled whenever he came close. I had a feeling she just liked spooking him; the big guy jumped when she bared her teeth.

I drew a dagger from my jacket, double checked it wasn't a prop knife—I'd made that mistake once, and Ryvan never let me live it down—and then rapped on the wooden door with the base of it.

"Housekeeping," I called in a sing-song voice.

Movement came from inside, more than one person scrabbling around.

*Get ready,* I warned my jaguar. I really needed to name her. *What about Tina?* I asked.

She shot me an image of her upper lip peeled back in a snarl.

*Malinda?* I tried.

More snarling.

I hammered on the door again. "It's rude to keep your guests waiting."

Around the back of the house, I heard a door slam open. Not very smart; they weren't even trying to be quiet.

*Rip their hamstrings,* I told Brenda. No—Dagger.

She growled in pure, hateful defiance. Definitely *not* Dagger.

I used the base of my knife to bash in the door handle and let myself into the house, scanning the small sitting room and kitchen. It was a single room, presumably with a bedroom and bathroom upstairs, and cluttered with too-big furniture. Whatever rebels lived here were gone; I veered upstairs to double check, but that too was empty.

My jaguar sent an image of three men writhing on the floor.

*Good job, Valour,* I praised, jogging back downstairs and through the back door.

When I reached them, my jaguar was purring, sitting on her haunches while she groomed her glowing body with a paw. The three humans groaned and cried on the ground, trying to crawl away.

"Valour, huh?" I asked, reaching out to pat my best girl on her head. She was made of magic; my hand should have passed all the way through. But she was strangely solid, and velvety like she had real fur. "Good job catching them. I'll take it from here."

Her eyes flashed with excitement if I wasn't mistaken, and she trotted a few paces away where she plopped down to watch.

"*So,* gentlemen," I said to the rebels, tossing my knife into the air and catching it easily. "Who wants to die first?"

"Who are you?" the one who'd lit the match in the coliseum growled. His brown hair had been burned on one side; aww, did his own fire get out of hand?

I knelt beside him, sneering as he tried to crawl away. It was more *slither away* with how badly Valour had savaged his calves.

"I was hoping you'd recognise me," I lamented. "I was on the stage earlier. Picture me with my hair up in a pretty chignon, my cheeks bright pink, and my lips red. Oh, and I was in a truly *atrocious* dress. It's got scorch marks all over it now."

"You're—the queen," a smaller man rasped, dragging himself along the ground, his dark eyes so wide I could see the whites. His left foot had been ripped off entirely. "From the play."

I snapped my fingers and pointed at him. "Bingo."

The third of their little trio—man, I was getting flashbacks to the three goblins who tried to eat me; why did everything come in threes?—pulled himself up against the side of a building and panted, watching me warily. He had a decent chunk taken out of his thigh, blood spurting from it. Judging by the resignation on his face, he knew it was a killing blow.

"What do you want?" he asked wearily.

"Glad you asked," I replied, more chipper than I felt deep down. "I'm here to get revenge for my friend. Zaugustus Agnes. He burned to death today thanks to the fire you set."

"Goblin?" the scrawny bastard with the burned hair asked, and when I nodded, he spat on the ground. "Piece of shit deserved to die."

Rage filled my chest on my next breath, pure and undiluted, and I crossed the ground between me and the *real* piece of shit in a rush. I took immense pleasure in stomping my boot down on his chest, the cracks of breaking ribs fuelling my wrath. He screamed so loudly there was no doubt someone would hear. I had to make this quick.

"Here's the real truth," I seethed, applying more pressure until more bones snapped. "Not all goblins are evil. Not all humans are good. Most humans I've met are somewhere in between, and a scary amount of them are black-hearted villains. You don't get to say someone deserves to die because of their species. If that's the case, all humans deserve to be wiped off the map."

He laughed.

Fuck him.

I drove my knife through the wreckage of his lungs, and pierced his heart. When I stood, the other two were staring at me like I was a monster.

"See?" I huffed. "Not all humans are good guys. I just killed a man. Now, which of you wants to die next?"

The small, one-footed man renewed his efforts to crawl away. I sighed.

"Your problem," I told him, kicking the dead bastard aside and stalking to my next victim, "is I only need one of you alive."

"Don't—" he began to plead.

"Don't what?" I interrupted, kicking his bloody ankle and drawing a violent scream from him. "Don't hurt you? You want me to show you the mercy you didn't show my friend? The mercy you showed *none* of the players? We were there to *act,* to put on a damn show, and you let us burn. Zaugustus was no harm to anyone, and he died because of your bullshit agenda."

The man gurgled with pain.

"You don't deserve mercy. Burning that theatre didn't help the war. It didn't save a single human. It achieved *nothing.*"

I gritted my teeth and dragged the sharp edge of my knife across his throat. I knew I was a bad person, but I would *never* set a fire and leave innocents to die. I'd never let people get caught in the crossfire and die needlessly. I might have been morally charcoal, but at least I wasn't pitch black.

And with that positive thought in mind, I turned to torture the final member of their little gang. Where the rest I'd seen earlier had gone, I couldn't guess. But I'd find them; sooner or later.

"I want to know two things," I said, crouching in front of the man bleeding out across the floor.

He nodded, like he wasn't surprised I planned to interrogate him. Smart man.

"Did you ever work with Natasya Stellara?"

His eyes flashed darker, a muscle clenching in his jaw. "Why do you want to know?"

"So that's a yes," I mused, ignoring the spasm in my heart. "You were the ones who sent her to steal the stone of power. You encouraged her to kill an eight year old. You killed a *kid*. And then because of you, that kid's brother killed *her*."

I drew a hard breath, nostrils flaring, my whole body trembling with rage.

"Second question. *Why?*"

I nudged his bleeding leg when he stayed silent, and he gritted his teeth against a howl of pain.

"We're not winning the war!" he blurted, pain making him wild. I removed my foot, flexing my fingers on my knife. "We've only held on this long because we stole magic from the goblin stores, but the objects of power are depleted, and with the fog over here killing goblins, there's nothing left to steal. We're losing. What other options do we have?"

I sucked in a slow breath, processing that little titbit. Celandrine hadn't told us we were losing, that was for sure.

"So you thought, 'how can we get an advantage? I know! Let's steal an object keeping a ten-year-old alive.'"

He shook his head, his jaw clenched.

"Did it help?" I pressed, so livid I shook. "The stone you stole? Did it make such a *huge* difference? Did it win the war? Are we all safe now?"

He was silent, panting through his pain.

*"Well?"* I demanded, a ruthless edge entering my voice.

"No!" he snapped. "It did nothing."

"Two people are dead because of that useless mission."

I contemplated my knife, wanting to cause maximum pain. "I lost my sister because of it. I want to know names. Everyone involved. Everyone you answer to."

Killing Kier wasn't going to grant me revenge. He'd lost as much as me; he was every bit as alone, twisted with grief, and ruled by hatred. But killing the band of rebels who'd sent Natasya to his castle in the first place? That was vengeance I deserved.

"I can't tell you names," the man rasped, his eyes flickering with agony. I added insult to injury—literally—by jostling his wound with the top of my boot. "I can't! She—bound us. We can't speak of it."

I crouched slowly, my heart beating hard, my pulse loud in my ears. "She, who?"

He shook his head weakly, sweat sticking his hair to his face. "We tried to stop this months ago, after we lost Natasya. We were—this was supposed to help us win the war, but it—it's out of control. She's got us by the balls."

"This mysterious *she* won't let you stop?"

He shook his head in confirmation, panting faster. "Tried. Failed. She hooked her command deeper. We never—wanted to work for her. Didn't realise who until—too late. We're supposed to kill goblins, not help them."

Hmm. I'd never heard of magic being able to compel someone, but then again I was human and my knowledge of magic was spotty at best. The idea of someone out there being able to command me against my will made my blood run cold.

"Who is she?" I pressed, jumping when the wind off the river ruffled my hair. Valour would have acted if someone tried to sneak up on me, but paranoia was setting in and overriding logic. "What's her name?"

The dying man laughed, shaking his head. "Can't tell

you. Wish I could; she deserves you to hunt her down and kill her. But I can't. And she'd control you, too."

That's what I was afraid of. But I had a magic jaguar and I was an assassin; even if she was some super powerful mob boss, surely, I stood a chance.

"Give me other names, then," I barked. "Tell me something useful and I'll make your death quick."

He laughed, his eyes glazed with pain. "They're my family. I won't sell them out."

I exhaled hard, frustration making me itchy. I had revenge for Zaugustus, and he had the justice he deserved, but this man knew something useful. This mysterious woman was a threat, and a damned deadly one. If I could leave here with information, that would be even better than vengeance.

"But I can—tell you she sent us to kill her own people," he rasped, his voice growing weaker but the glint in his eyes harder than before. "She wants all goblins to bow to her; the fog plays into her plans. She probably made it."

*Or* it was the physical manifestation of Kier's grief over losing Danette. Definitely one or the other.

*"Listen,"* he groaned, catching my stare. "She sent us to kill her own people."

"Got it," I agreed. "That's completely useless, but thanks. I need a name."

He laughed, his eyes rolling to the dark sky. "Her people. Listen."

I grabbed his shoulder and dug my fingers in. "Tell me *her name.*"

His breathing came faster, harder, and his eyes rolled in his skull. He opened his mouth—and nothing came out.

"Cl—" he forced out, the word strangling him—

Blood exploded up his throat and splattered my boots.

"What the fuck?" I gasped, reaching for him and releasing a deep, guttural growl when I saw the emptiness in his eyes.

He'd tried to fight the magic binding him, and it had killed him.

"Well, I promised you a quick death," I sighed, closing his eyes with my fingertips.

And he'd set the coliseum on fire, so he deserved the pain and suffering. He'd killed Zaugustus with his actions.

*But he was compelled,* a traitorous voice pointed out.

I sighed and turned away from the carnage I'd created, giving Valour a look and patting the ring on my chest. She stretched and rose with a long yawn, like she was more than ready to return to my ring and take a nap.

*Thanks for your help,* I told her.

She headbutted my knee before she leapt, transforming back into glowing blue magic and vanishing into my ring.

*She bound us. She sent us to kill her own people.*

Her own people—goblins? Their puppet master wasn't human; she was a goblin.

"So," I murmured, quickly leaving the scene of the crime before goblin police found me. If Greenheart even had coppers. "There's a powerful goblin out there compelling human rebels to do her dirty work. And killing her own species, too."

She wasn't just deadly; she was ruthless if she didn't mind killing her own kind. But to what end? He mentioned she wanted *all* goblins under her control, which suggested she already had a following. A general in the army, maybe?

But if the goblins were beating humans in the war, why was she amassing power?

If she was Greenheart, the answer was obvious. She wanted Bluescale lands, too. Their rivalry was legend, and the border between the two realms was fraught with assaults and skirmishes.

But why use humans?

*We're supposed to kill goblins, not help them.*

Unless she didn't want the attacks to be linked to her. Sending rebels to kill her people could stir up discontent here, in Greenheart. To give people a taste of blood so they craved the battle. And then she could blame it on their goblin rivals, and give them a reason to hate Bluescale.

The biggest question: did this woman compel Natasya to steal the stone of power keeping Danette alive? Did she use unwitting humans to kill Kier's sister?

And if that was the case, what the hell was I going to do with this information?

Uncomfortably close behind me, a bell began to ring, filling the night with noise.

Shit, someone had found the bodies faster than I'd planned.

I pulled my collar up around my face, ducked my head, and walked faster through the dark goblin town.

# 7

*I* let out a low whistle at the huge columns flanking the imposing gates to Emeran, the Greenheart capital. Two jade dragons were carved around the columns, so realistic I half expected their spiked tails to snap in our directions, or for the immense teeth in their open jaws to snap shut around us.

"What's with all the dragons?" I asked Cherish. "There were loads of them in Bluescale, too."

She gave me a dead-eyed look, her brows in a deep V as she sipped tea from a chipped bottle. She'd lost a friend and come on her period all within twelve hours; she was reasonably in a foul mood. "You seriously don't know?"

"I seriously don't," I confirmed, following the broad shape of Hames's back up the steep path into the city.

"Our goddess is Gaia, the Mother of All Things," she explained, still giving me that flat look.

"Yeah..." I knew that much, at least.

"Gaia is a dragon," she said, as if I was stupid for not knowing that.

"Ohhhh, so your goddess is a dragon. Hence the

dragon-y stuff everywhere to honour her. Got it. Wait, you swear by saying *Gaia's tits.* How does a dragon have tits?"

"All dragons have tits, you fool," Jakoda snapped, hurrying to catch up to us. "Now shut your mouths, both of you. Emeran isn't kind to humans *or* goblins in human forms, so Letta and Ryvan, you need to behave. No killing anyone."

I widened my eyes, all innocence.

Did she know I'd hunted down the humans who set the fire? It was hard to tell; the woman had a killer poker face.

"Stay with one of the others at all times," she went on in a hard command. "These people don't like Bluescale much either, so be on your guard. And don't say anything idiotic. Don't insult anyone's mother, don't challenge someone to arm wrestling, don't even look them in the eyes."

"Whole lotta *don'ts* there, Jak," Ryvan quipped, but his voice was flatter than usual, grief crushing the vibrancy from him.

Jakoda snapped her sharp teeth at him. "Behave, or I'll eat your heart myself."

I shot Ryvan a stunned look. She wasn't serious about heart-eating, right? That wasn't a thing goblins actually *did.* Right?

But he ducked his head, his mouth pressed thin, and didn't open his smart mouth again. Shit, she was serious.

"We're here for three hours to stock up on supplies," our new leader reminded us as we climbed the hill towards the looming gates—and the city full of goblins who wanted to eat me and kill everyone else. "We go in, get our shit, and get out. Understood?"

I nodded. Ryvan bobbed his head too. Hames gave Jakoda a curt, "Yes, ma'am."

"I guess," Aerona muttered.

Cherish was silent, glaring up at the city.

"Cherish," Jakoda prompted, aiming a stern look that melted into worry at the younger woman.

"I heard you," Cherish replied flatly. "I won't start trouble."

"Good girl," Jakoda replied, giving her a semi-comforting whack on the shoulder. "We're in, out, then back to the camp. This won't take long."

I raised my eyebrows. Famous last words.

FOR SOME MYSTERIOUS REASON, Jakoda partnered me with Hames, who was even surlier and quieter than usual. And that was saying something.

We'd managed to successfully buy a length of canvas and thread to shore up the holes in our tents, and procured an absurd quantity of matches. Zaugustus always started our fires; the rest of us were hopeless. It was a sobering thing to need matches at all.

I took Jakoda's advice and avoided eye contact with the Greenheart goblins as much as I could, keeping my head down and making sure I didn't accidentally bump into someone and start a brawl.

"What's got you so quiet?" I asked Hames, glancing over my shoulder and unable to shake the sense that someone was watching us.

But we were Bluescale goblins—and a human—in the Greenheart capital. Of course people watched us; we stood out.

"Nothing," Hames muttered, his deep blue hands curling into fists as he scanned the market around us for the food section. We had orders to buy anything dried, tinned, or preserved.

"I totally believe that," I quipped, spotting a stall with half a cow hanging on a hook. Perfect. "Look, there's dried meat."

Hames muttered under his breath but stuck close to my side as we wove around the stalls, his hands pale-knuckled on the length of canvas.

Abruptly, he blurted, "Cherish wants to marry me."

I snapped my head around to stare at him, my mouth dropping open. "Then marry her, man! Have you *seen* that woman? She's gorgeous. I'm surprised she doesn't have droves of admirers trying to win her hand."

Hames's mouth pressed thin, his nostrils flaring. "She did. That's why she joined the troupe; to escape them."

I processed that. It made sense; Cherish wasn't a huge fan of men.

"But she likes *you?*" I asked, and tried not to sound too surprised.

Hames was gloomy and silent, and spent most of his time building his muscles or brooding by himself. He was great for moving furniture, and loyal to a fault, but I wouldn't have called him a heartthrob. My mistake.

"She doesn't *like* me," he disagreed, glaring at a Greenheart kid who ran in front of us, chased by his mother. "She wants to marry me for safety, so we can get a house and—all of that," he finished, waving a hand.

The man was both blind and hopeless.

"She always sticks close to you, though," I pointed out, dodging the pursuing mother as she held out a flip-flop in a warning to her son.

"Because I'm bigger and scare off predators," Hames replied glumly, his gold rings catching the light as his fingers curled into a fist.

"And she gave you that syrup bread last week, remember?"

"Because Zaugustus told her to," he growled—but his scowl froze as he seemed to remember the old man was gone. "She wants safety, not me. I don't know why she doesn't ask someone else."

I gave the big guy a dry look as we approached the dried meat vendor, the smell of it reaching me before I ever saw the big, green woman selling the food. Cherish had a sharp tongue and a pretty face, but deep down she was full of anxiety. It was why she always smelled like tea leaves and mint; the infusion calmed her nerves. So did Hames, not that he'd ever notice.

"You do the talking," I told him, angling my head at the vendor. He huffed a long-suffering sigh and approached the woman, buying our meat.

The feeling that we were being watched intensified, burning the back of my neck. I turned, discreetly scanning the market as Hames and the woman negotiated a price. Huge men and women filled the spaces between stalls, their arms and packs full of wares.

Beyond the flat roofs of the market, dark buildings cluttered the streets with sharp chimneys billowing grey smoke into the sky. Above it all, the vicious castle loomed, like something out of a nightmare. If this was a fairytale, the wicked witch would live there, cooking children in a giant pot in front of the fire. No one spoke of the Green-heart queen, not a single word. Either she was the most boring woman alive, or the most heinous.

In the market, no one watched us with more than

passing curiosity or disdain. But Jakoda was right that Emeran's residents were less than fond of their blue rivals, and even less of human-looking folk like me. A woman with an impressive nose and a scarred cheek snapped her teeth at me, and licked her lips when she noticed my attention. But she was no more interested in me than the three bastards who'd wanted to eat me behind the inn.

But still, I felt watched.

"What is it?" Hames asked, hefting a giant bundle of meat onto his other shoulder. With a sigh, I took the canvas off him so he wasn't a *total* pack horse.

"Not a clue," I replied warily, meeting his soulful dark eyes. "But someone's watching us; I can feel it."

"I felt so, too," he admitted, his broad features sharpening. "Come on, let's find the others and get out of this city."

"The sooner the better," I muttered, knowing if our stalker showed themselves, I'd confront them, and there'd be no shortage of trouble. I'd promised Jakoda I wouldn't start shit, and we *all* deserved a peaceful afternoon after— after last night.

Fuck, Zaugustus was really gone.

"I won't let anyone hurt you," Hames said unprompted as we walked faster through the market, aiming for an emerald bridge where we'd promised to convene with the rest of our troupe. "No one will eat you while I'm with you."

I knocked my shoulder into his, dredging up a grin. "See, this is why Cherish likes you. Under all that scowling silence, you're actually pretty sweet."

He sighed, any openness leaving his expression. "I wish I'd been paired with Ryvan."

I snorted. That little shit? "No, you don't."

A tiny corner of Hames's dark blue mouth flickered. "Fine. No, I don't."

We walked the rest of the way in companionable silence, but there was no shaking the feeling of eyes following us the whole way.

# 8

Other than witnessing a goblin murdered outside a pub, we left Emeran without consequence. Jakoda assured us brawls and deaths were common, and even encouraged; the citizens were huge fans of *survival of the fittest.*

"Good riddance," I muttered under my breath as we left the big iron gates, the carved dragons watching us stumble down the hill with our arms full of supplies.

The further we walked from Emeran, the less the back of my neck burned, and the sensation of being watched faded. I allowed myself to relax, and gave Hames a pointed look when Cherish moved around Aerona to walk by his side. She'd been breathing in tight, short breaths for an hour, but I kept an eye on her, curious to know if I was right. By the time we got back to our camp, her breaths were long and full, and there was something calmer to her expression.

Did it even matter if she liked him? Wasn't a sense of safety a good enough reason to marry?

Maybe I was focusing on the wrong person; maybe Hames didn't like *her*. He certainly never showed it in his stony expression if he did.

"Don't meddle," Ryvan chided so only I could hear him. "You don't like when people get involved in your love life; give them the same courtesy."

I widened my eyes. "But I don't *have* a love life."

Ryvan's tanned face narrowed with wryness. *"Sure,"* he agreed, completely falsely, and jogged ahead to help Jakoda organise our purchases.

With a scowl, and the reminder of my hateful husband at the forefront of my mind, I stalked around the circle of tents and disappeared into mine.

I only emerged to eat dinner, and when I saw the vat of dark, fragrant broth with strange, little pastry boats floating in it, I wished I hadn't.

*You've never seen dumpling soup before?*

Kier's laughter taunted me, filling my ears, tightening my heart.

"Here," Cherish said, and then huffed, "Letta," when I didn't realise she was talking to me.

I accepted the offering, and stared at the bowl of soup and floating dumplings with dread. I felt sick. My chest ached viciously, the mate bond slicing with a sudden pain. It took all my concentration to lock down a gasp at the razor-sharp sensation.

*I don't miss him,* I growled at the bond. *He can rot in Hell for all I care.*

I grabbed a spoon and slurped up soup out of pure spite.

Aerona gave me a strange look when I angrily bit into a dumpling—and struggled *so damn hard* to hold onto my rage when flavours and soft textures wrapped around my tongue. They were good. The evil, floating dumplings were *good* and for some reason, that made me want to cry.

I wished I was back on the rooftop of Kier's castle, with the wind brushing through my hair and his arms wrapped around me. Then, I'd been comforting him, but I wished he were here now to comfort *me*. I needed a hug, but mostly—mostly I just wanted my bastard mate.

It wasn't fair. I wasn't supposed to love him; I wasn't supposed to long for him so badly my chest stabbed and the bond throbbed with physical pain.

*Get over it, Zaba,* I growled at myself, viciously eating more dumplings. *He doesn't want you. You hate him. Just move on.*

Of course, I only realised a moment later that I'd given myself the name Kier called me.

*Don't cry. Don't you dare cry.*

I tipped the bowl to my mouth and swallowed the last of the soup, just to hide my face as I dug claws into my composure and pulled it back together.

"I want to say something," Aerona murmured when we were finished, the six of us sitting in strange silence for long moments.

She put her bowl down and stood, taking her jet hair from the pigtails she wore to make herself look young and harmless. With her hair in wild curls and a hardness to her expression, I saw her for the first time. Young, but fierce, honed into a deadly blade by the streets she'd lived on for years. It was like looking into a mirror.

"I know I give you guys shit about being embarrassing and I act like I don't like you but—" She took a tough breath, crossing her arms over her chest and staring into the fire in the middle of our camp. "You guys are my family, and Zaugustus was family, too. He was a good man. The world is so fucked up with him gone."

I nodded, my jaw clenched to ward off any more emotion.

"I wanted to say that—that I love you, and I don't want to lose anyone else. So no one do anything stupid, okay?"

Cherish flew up from her seat on the ground and wrangled Aerona into a hug. Tears streaked her cobalt face, clinging to her long lashes.

Aerona hugged her for long moments before lifting her head off Cherish's shoulder. "And if *any* of you repeat what I just said, or even *think* about bringing it up, I'll slit all your throats in your sleep."

"And she's back," Ryvan laughed, silver lining his eyes as he smiled. "You fuckers are my family, too."

Hames grunted his agreement, colour on his cheeks but desolation in his eyes.

In the pause, I murmured, "I don't know where I'd be without you." It was the truth, and not something I wanted to think about. "No one else would be mad enough to take in a human and treat her like their own."

"Not to mention an assassin," Jakoda added, fondness softening the edge from her eyes, telling me she was joking.

"Exactly," I agreed, ignoring the emotion that clogged in my throat. "I can kill anyone you want gone. If that's not family, I don't know what is."

But there was no hiding the hurt that sat among us like a seventh member, occupying the same space Zaugustus had.

"I'm going to sleep," Cherish said with a sniffle,

squeezing Aerona into another hug before letting the girl go.

"You didn't finish your soup," I pointed out, her bowl still half full.

"I'm fine," she dismissed, summoning a watery smile as she headed to her tent.

I nudged Ryvan, because he was the closest to me. "You should take the bowl to her. She's upset."

"No shit," he muttered, bracing his hands on the floor to push to his feet.

"I'll take it," Hames offered, his voice low and quiet. He scooped up the bowl in his big hands before Ryvan could get there, and disappeared into Cherish's tent with her.

"I'm off, too. I want to sharpen my knives," Aerona murmured, which was code for *cry in private.*

I knew the feeling; pressure had built behind my eyes and nose and remained there, making my eyes burn. I glanced at my empty bowl, the dumpling soup I'd devoured, and wanted to weep.

I cleaned my bowl and left it near the fire when I retreated to my tent, but I sat in the doorway while everyone bundled themselves inside newly repaired tents. The cold air felt good against my hot face as I finally let the tears fall, my bottom lip wobbling like a drunk seagull in a storm.

I covered my face when a fresh wave of emotion rushed, hot, from my eyes, and when I lowered my hands, low-slung fog had glided around the camp, obscuring the base of each tent, hiding the bowls we'd left around the fire.

I jumped to my feet with a gasp, but the fog wasn't destroying the tents, and no one screamed like they had in Cyana.

A tremor went through my belly; my bottom lip wobbled again.

I ducked back into my tent, grabbed my weapons and my coat, and followed the flow of the fog.

The Haar was here, but why?

# 9

*I* found him sitting on a log a few minutes away, moonlight breaking through the tall green trees to dapple his opaque white body with silver. His form was stronger than before, every shape of him defined, like I was looking at Kier himself. Well, if someone had thrown a tin of white paint over him.

He lifted his head when I purposely crunched a twig, but with his mist covering the ground, he probably felt every move I made.

Wordlessly, the Haar held a hand out to me, and like a true masochist, I put my hand in his without hesitation and sat beside him.

"Why are you here?" I murmured, not wanting to break the silence but needing to know.

"Hurts," he replied just as quietly, lifting his free hand to his chest, over his heart. "Here. Zaba hurts."

I sucked in a surprised breath. The trembling thing in my belly weakened further, somewhere between sickness and butterflies.

"You can feel the mate bond?"

He was growing more Kier every time I saw him, and I didn't know what to think of that. Did the man weaken as the grief grew stronger?

"Have you—seen Kier?" I asked tentatively, glancing at his profile. "The other Kier, I mean."

The Haar shook his pale head, his fingers flexing around my hand. "Stay close to Zaba."

I blinked, processing that. "You've been following me?"

I wasn't as alarmed by that as I should have been. Comfort unfurled through my soul instead.

He nodded, white hair dancing with the motion. "Safe."

He had a point. I'd needed to be rescued from three goblins who wanted to eat me, after all.

"Thanks," I murmured, unable to stop myself adding, "But I can handle myself, Kier. I'm an assassin for gods' sakes."

The Haar just watched me, his eyes narrowed. Probably thinking I was a hypocrite for condemning him for killing people when I was a killer, too. But at least I didn't murder indiscriminately.

"Does Kier—the other one—know you're here? Can he—hear me?"

He blinked milky white eyes, either unsure of the question or the answer.

"Kier," he said, something chasing across his face. "Kier hurt Zaba."

I blew out a hard breath, staring at the tree canopy high above, trying to block out the painful memories.

"Yeah, but Zaba hurt Kier, too. I tried to murder him; I'm hardly innocent. He shouldn't have exiled me, though."

The Haar watched me sadly, his thumb brushing my knuckles.

"You know what really pisses me off?" I asked, now I had someone who knew exactly what had happened, and who was strangely *easy* to talk to, unlike Ryvan. "What must the people of Lazankh think, when one day I'm there and the next I'm gone? They must think I abandoned them like a coward, probably ran back to Lucre to escape the—fog."

Nearly said *Haar,* but that seemed rude.

"So he kicked me out of my home, renounced me as his wife, *and* made me look like a coward in one fell swoop. Bastard," I snarled.

"Bastard," Kier repeated with feeling.

"Yeah, that's you, buddy," I laughed. "Kinda. I don't know how much blame you should get for the other Kier's actions. But I'm pissed at you, too. Stop destroying cities; those are people's *homes.*"

"Homes," he muttered, staring at the canopy of leaves above us with a furrow pinching his brow. "Not safe."

"And murder is *totally* safe," I drawled.

"Not kill," he threw back, some of Kier's signature grumpiness narrowing the Haar's eyes. "Save."

"Semantics," I replied, waving my hand. Sure, you kill to save people from this cruel world, but they're still *dead.* "Listen, there's something you should know. You *and* the other Kier. The rebels who stole the stone of power and killed Danette are still active. A group of them set a theatre on fire in Verna and—"

The Haar leapt to his feet with a deep, guttural growl that raised the fine hairs on the back of my neck. The fingers that had been soft and blunt moments ago tore from mine and tipped with long, vicious claws. He bared many teeth, the sight chilling my blood.

Okay, so I should have realised Danette was a touchy subject.

"Dead," the Haar seethed, his chest rising and falling fast. "Kier killed them. All of them."

"Well, some of them didn't die," I sighed, watching fog thicken around his feet, "or there were more of them than you realised."

"Still active," he growled, the fog he was formed of seeming to pulse, like he was a creature of magic and *fury* instead of magic and grief.

"Yup. My troupe got caught in the theatre blaze and we —we lost someone."

The rough burr of emotion in my voice made the Haar pause, and he strode back to the log to—to pull me into a tight hug.

I melted into the embrace, my head falling onto his shoulder and a breath punching from my lungs. I wasn't willing to admit how badly I'd needed this, and how much I wanted Kier—the other Kier, the bastard who snarled and glared and brooded like his life depended on it. The bastard who didn't want me.

Tears dripped down my cheeks and here, alone with him, I let them.

"Be honest," I murmured against the Haar's shoulder. "What are my chances of talking some sense into Kier if I sneak back into Lazankh? Think he'll kill me, or kiss me?"

"Not hurt," Haar replied, his voice low and soft. Fingers carded through my hair, cold and gentle. "Never."

*Never* was optimistic. He'd told everyone to murder me if I ever stepped foot in the city again. But if the troupe's path ever returned to the city ... maybe I'd scale the balcony in disguise and pay my husband a visit.

Maybe I'd hold a knife to his throat and recreate my dream.

I lifted my head off the Haar's shoulder with a sigh, feeling more settled than I had before, my worries and doubts quieter. But I inhaled sharply when a bright orange glow drew my attention deeper through the forest. In the direction I'd come from.

*"Ruthless gods, no.* Is that a fire?"

I couldn't breathe. I was going to throw up.

He let me go as we both rose from the log, the Haar spinning to look where I pointed and a low sound rumbling from his chest.

"Stay," he ordered. "Zaba, safe."

I shook my head hard, already stalking across the clearing, panic driving me. "I'm not a damsel, Kier. And my friends are camped in that direction; I need to warn them. Besides, how are you going to put out a fire? You're literal fog."

He shot me an arch look as he kept pace with me. "Fog can suffocate."

I ignored his growing vocabulary. "Yeah, well, my friends are sleeping in a camp nearby and if they see you, they'll freak out."

I didn't let him argue, pushing myself faster through the trees, narrowly avoiding tripping on tree roots that made the ground a treacherous maze.

The closer I got to the camp, the bigger the orange glow became, and smoke joined the fog in the forest. My heart tripped between frantic beats. The fire wasn't just close to our camp; our camp was burning.

When I skidded out of the tree line, my stomach revolted so suddenly I tasted bile.

"Go," I hissed at Kier without turning. "Get out of here."

My troupe raced frantically through the flames, gathering things in their arms, getting our meagre possessions out of the path of the fire. Ryvan's tent was burning. So was mine

"What the hell happened?" I demanded, leaping a burning piece of fabric and landing beside Cherish.

"Where were you?" she demanded, her eyes flashing.

"I needed some air," I replied shortly, quickly assessing what could be saved. "Losing a friend will do that to you."

Her expression softened. "Sorry about your tent. We tried to save it, but it was already spreading.

"It's fine," I sighed. It wasn't. All my possessions had been inside it, and now I was back to square one. Exactly like when I left Lazankh with only the clothes on my back. "Who set the fire? And where are Hames and Aerona?"

"They ran after the bastards who torched our camp," Ryvan spat, dumping an armful of things outside the fire while Jakoda dumped water on a blaze.

I reached into the grass to salvage our jar of water, and hissed when the pot burned my fingers, dropping it back to the ground.

"Careful," I snapped at Ryvan, grabbing his arm and pulling him from the path of an errant stream of flame. This was deliberate—every bit as deliberate as the theatre blaze. "Are we being targeted? First the coliseum, and now our camp—"

I cut off when a deep, throaty roar cut the night, and I snapped my head up in panic, waiting for the Haar's furious form to come storming out of the dark cluster of trees with the arsonists in hand. Instead, I let out a slow breath when Aerona and Hames appeared, throwing a deep, forest green bastard with impressive horns and a slim, snake-like face to the ground. His hand landed in a patch of fire and he screeched.

I winced; I knew the feeling. My hand throbbed, smarting where I'd grabbed the hot jar. I flexed it, the skin pink and shiny.

Jakoda strode around the fire towards the goblin Aerona had shoved, a low, rumbling laugh in the back of her throat. It sent a shudder down my spine, reminiscent of so many psychopaths I'd known in Seagrave. Hell, most of Marc the Scythe's gang had been terrifying, and Jakoda managed to unsettle me more than all of them put together.

The green bastard surged up like he thought he could flee despite five goblins and a human surrounding him, but I grasped the ring hanging from my chain and imagined giving my jaguar a little scratch under her chin.

*Wanna hunt, Valour?*

She leapt out of the ring with a growl that chilled even my blood, and pounced on the goblin before he could get further than a foot. I grinned, showing off and shameless about it.

Hames gave me a wary look like he always did when Valour came out to play. Apparently, I should have needed more gemstones to summon power this big. Oh, and I was human. I shouldn't have had power at all.

"Answer my questions, or this beast will rip your head off," Jakoda warned in a deep, chilling voice. "And I'll let her devour your skull for a crunchy snack."

I grinned. Nice. Jakoda was truly a terrifying being, and I loved it. The arsonist didn't love it so much. The whites of his eyes showed, and he tried to crawl backwards. Failed, obviously.

"First question," Jakoda growled, her wrinkled blue face cruel and wrathful. "Why did you torch our camp?"

"Bluescale aren't wanted here," he spat. "The queen's orders. You're all spies for the royal bastards."

I exchanged a glance with Ryvan. We knew Bluescale weren't welcome in the capital, but there were no warnings of being torched if we lingered.

"That bitch," Hames snarled, his blue hands curling into fists and his whole body shaking. "She won't stop until we're all dead. I say we go to the castle now and torch it, see how she likes it."

"Whoa, buddy," I replied, my eyes wide at his fervency. "Let's not make any hasty suicide plans, yeah?"

Storming the Greenheart castle was a one-way ticket to the afterlife. That building was *huge,* and from what Jakoda told us, armed to the teeth.

"First she released the Haar, and now *this,"* Hames went on, his voice deep and vibrating. He made to stalk away, but Cherish stepped into his path, her palms held out to him.

"If you go to the castle, you'll never come back."

"So?" he demanded, tendons standing out on his neck. "There's no one waiting for me to come home. If I go, I can kill her and finally rid the world of that threat."

"I'd be waiting," Cherish said in a small voice, her brows pinched with pain.

Hames swallowed, his nostrils flaring. But he stayed put and said nothing as Jakoda continued to interrogate the bastard we'd captured.

"Did you follow us from the capital?" Jakoda pressed,

Valour snarling into the bastard's face. "Or were you sent for us specifically?"

"We follow all Bluescale in the capital," he gasped in pain. "You were stupid to come here. Go back to your kingdom."

How boringly xenophobic. *Give him a little nip,* I told Valour.

She bared her sharp, blue teeth and sank them deep into his shoulder, making the man scream.

When Ryvan and Cherish swung stares on me, I widened my eyes. "Oopsie."

"How do you have magic?" Hames muttered, but mostly to himself.

"Who cares how?" I replied, my pulse slamming in my throat at the violence in the air. "Just be glad I do. I don't see you summoning your own power."

His mouth pressed thin, big arms crossed over his chest. "My magic could bring down a tree; it's not safe."

"As opposed to the fire raging through the camp behind us," I drawled but without heat. "Do we have everything we need to know from this guy?" I asked Jakoda.

She blew a rough breath out of her nostrils and nodded. "Unless you want to tell us anything else useful."

"You're inferior to us Greenheart goblins. Look at our cities and power compared to yours—"

*Rip out his throat,* I ordered Valour. She complied with relish and a low growl-purr in her chest.

"So, we're being hunted by Bluescale guards because we're rebellious little shits, and now we've got Greenheart to add to the list," I sighed, looking at my troupe. "Anyone else? The human armies wanna come try to kill us?"

"Don't tempt fate," Aerona hissed, and I realised the girl had been uncommonly quiet. I eyed her suspiciously, my eyes snagging on the delicate way she held herself. *Shit.*

"Show me," I ordered, crunching branches and blackened leaves underfoot as I stalked over to her. "Where are you hurt?"

"I'm fine," she snarled, teeth bared. She kept her arms tight to her side, her posture stiff.

"I said," I repeated firmly, *"show me."*

Her turquoise eyes were tight with pain, her jaw clenched, but she must have known I wouldn't back down because she held her arm out to me.

I carefully turned her arm so I could see her forearm, and hissed out a breath at the red, angry path of a burn. Fuck, she must have been in excruciating agony.

"Hames," I barked, meeting his solemn eyes. "How are you at healing?"

"Passable," he replied seriously, striding to us and peering at Aerona's injury. "I'm better with pain relief," he added softly, a reassuring smile on his dark blue face as he met Aerona's tight glare. I let go of her arm and gave them space when the many rings and bracelets Hames wore began to glow. Aerona sagged with visible relief.

"Pack up everything we can salvage," Jakoda barked at the rest of us, walking around the dead goblin on the ground. "We need to get out of here."

"We're going back to Bluescale?" Ryvan asked, staring at the older woman in surprise.

"No," she scoffed. "And let that tyrant bitch win? I don't think so. But we need to get word out to all the Bluescale in this kingdom. Everyone needs to lie low until it's safe to go home."

My eyes strayed to the edge of the forest, where the

Haar waited out of sight. I could feel him even if I couldn't see him. He had the power to end this, to make Bluescale safe, to stop hurting people. But he refused. And while I let him soothe my ragged bond, and comfort my soul, wasn't I condoning that murder?

The next time I saw him, he needed an ultimatum.

*Stop killing, or you'll never see me again.*

I just didn't know what it would do to me if he chose murder over me. He was the only part of Kier I had left, and I was stupidly attached to him.

I dragged my focus to Aerona's arm as Hames healed her, so I didn't have to think about losing the Haar when I'd already lost Natasya, Kier, and Zaugustus.

# 10

To sum everything up, Bluescale had sent their guards to arrest us because of the treason we committed in our plays; human rebels were hunting down all goblins because they were compelled by a mysterious woman; and now the Greenheart queen wanted Bluescale removed from her lands or burned to a crisp.

And *still,* somehow, this was more appealing than running back to Seagrave and pretending to hate goblins again.

"How many left?" I asked Jakoda, the old woman striding ahead at a pace so angry I had to jog to keep up.

We'd spent the morning visiting all the Bluescale goblins we'd settled here to escape the Haar, and warning them to lay low. Three hours of endless walking, and my body aching. I thought I'd conditioned myself to exercise after countless days of hiking through the forest between goblin kingdoms, but the strained muscles in my ass disagreed. Vehemently.

"Two in this city," Jakoda replied with a scowl on her

wrinkled blue face. "Presuming Ryvan and Aerona have done their job correctly."

"Debatable," I drawled, watching a robed man across the green-brick street, and wrapping my fingers around my ring in case he decided to attack us.

He didn't even look our way as he ducked inside one of the sturdy terrace houses and shut the door behind himself. Okay, so I was a tad paranoid.

"Here," Jakoda muttered, balling her clawed fingers into a fist and hammering on the dull wooden door like the family who lived here owed her money. "What?" she barked when she caught me staring at her.

"Did that door insult your mother?"

She rolled her eyes, giving only a throaty noise in answer.

"We don't want any trouble," a tall, slim goblin said when he opened the door, visibly cowering. "We—oh, Jakoda, it's you."

"Who else would it be?" she replied coarsely, putting her hands on her hips. The long coat she wore was singed in a few places, and so was the lacy skirt she had on underneath it. At least Jakoda wore a billion layers at once; she'd probably saved all her wardrobe by virtue of wearing it in its entirety while the fire blazed. "Friendly warning. Keep your head down, Kaegon. Greenhearts are kicking out any of us they find, so don't draw attention. Wear a glamour if you need to."

She spat every word with the same sharpness as my favourite dagger. *Friendly* warning? She ought to tell her voice that.

"What do you mean Greenhearts are *kicking us out?*" the man demanded, raising to his full height. "We came here for safety."

"I mean they're kicking us out," Jakoda growled in his face, uncowed. "It's not a complex statement. Be careful— and avoid the capital."

With that, she turned and stalked away.

"Sorry about her," I said, reaching out to pat the poor man's arm. "She's just extra snarly because she's worried and—"

"Letta," Jakoda barked, giving me a stern look from halfway down the road.

"Coming," I called, giving her a little wave. "She's right though, avoid the capital and keep your head down. Nice meeting you again. How's the wife?"

"She's—"

"*Now,* Letta," Jakoda yelled.

I gave the man an apologetic look and jogged to catch up to my prickly friend.

"Your bedside manner needs work," I told her. "Poor guy just got told he's not safe here *or* in Bluescale; you could try being a little..."

"What?" she demanded, an eyebrow raised.

"Sweeter?"

"Like you?"

"Ehh, fair point." I scanned the street, looking for anything out of place and finding a normal, residential street. "Where's the next family, then?"

"On the other side of that park." She pointed at a big green slope at the end of the road, with a knot of dense trees and a sad attempt at a sand pit for kids to play in next to a few benches. "What's going on with you and Ryvan?"

"Huh?"

"You're spending a lot of time together," she added slyly.

She thought we were an item?

*Wow.*

Without looking her in the eye, I said, "Four months ago, I married my enemy to kill him in revenge for murdering my sister. *But* because the universe is a bastard, I had to wait a month to murder him. During that time, I made the stupid mistake of falling in love with him."

"Gaia's great tits," she murmured as we crossed the road.

"*But*," I powered on, "the asshole still deserved to die, so I tried to slit his throat. I couldn't do it, because like I already mentioned, I loved him. Then he found out I was a liar and a fake, and he renounced me as his wife."

I looked Jakoda dead in the eye, my expression flat. "I hate him with all my heart, and I know he hates me too. But I can't stop loving him, even now. So no, there's nothing between me and Ryvan."

Jakoda just stared at me as we passed under the iron archway into the park, obviously struggling for a response.

"Right, then," she said eventually. "That's that."

"Yup."

She reached into her bag and rooted around, coming up with a lemon biscuit. When she thrust it at me, I accepted it wordlessly, biting into the sweet, bitter snack.

If I hadn't been so focused on my biscuit—and my painful memories—I might have noticed the five humans sneaking out of the treeline.

But I didn't see them until three went for Jakoda, moving so fast we were caught before we could fight. Only two grabbed me, which would be their undoing.

The moment rough hands pinched around my arms, I

reacted automatically, falling back on both training and survival instincts learned from the streets.

My foot slammed into their instep; my elbow rammed their ribs; and when one faltered and loosened their grip on me, I spun and drove me fist into the blunt face of the other man. Blood sprayed when his nose broke and I hammered my advantage, slamming my knuckles into his nose again. His roar of pain sawed my nerves like a blade.

What the hell was going on in this kingdom? Were these humans part of the same rebel band Natasya had worked for? Were they compelled?

"If someone is controlling you, blink twice," I said, backing up and warily scanning the park for Jakoda and her three assailants.

Shit, where were they? Had the old battle-axe really been overpowered?

The bastards who attacked me didn't blink twice, or at all. The first one who'd grabbed me came at me again, favouring one side thanks to his newly flat foot. I hoped it hurt like hell where I'd stomped on him.

"What do you bastards want?" I demanded, throwing a warning fist.

"We need humans like you," he replied, shocking me still for a moment. Damn, I hadn't expected him to speak. Or to know I was human; I was supposed to be a glamoured goblin.

"For *what?* If this is some freaky experiment, I'm sorry but I'll have to pass."

When he came a little close for comfort, I slammed my fist into his stomach and knocked the air out of him. On the plus side, they weren't trying to kill me so that gave me an advantage. Because I was definitely trying to kill *them.*

"We lost members recently," the one whose nose I'd broken mumbled, his voice thick with blood. "We need to replenish our numbers."

They'd lost members? Wow, who knew? Definitely not me who killed three of them.

"Yeah, well, you bastards killed one of my friends so forgive me if I'm not sympathetic," I snarled, and grabbed my ring.

*Kill them all,* I told Valour, a blue glow blasting from under my fingers and—faltering when pain pricked my neck.

Shit, I *knew* that prick. Nothing good ever came from being jabbed with a needle.

"Motherfuckers," I snarled, twisting and ripping the syringe out of my neck. The liquid was green and transparent. Either madflower, which sent someone so crazy they usually killed themselves by accident, or sleeproot. And since they didn't want me dead, my money was on the latter.

"I'm going to kill every single one of you," I slurred, gritting my teeth when the park blurred and twisted around me. Oh, goody, it was a highly concentrated dose. "Every single one," I reiterated, curling my fingers into a fist around my ring and swearing when the glow of power cut out.

"A human with magic," one of them murmured. "This could change everything."

"Change your insides to outsides," I threatened clumsily, my tongue thick in my mouth. I threw my fist in a pathetic punch. "You're so dead."

The ground rushed up so fast it blurred, but rough arms caught me before I could smack into it face first.

My last rational thought before I passed out was, *at*

*least I didn't knock out my teeth. I've gone twenty seven years without losing my teeth, and I'm not about to start now.*

# 11

"This is gonna sound really weird," I told Kier, my head resting on his shoulder while I sat on his lap on the castle rooftop, all of Lazankh spread out below us. "But I could've sworn I'd been kidnapped."

He stiffened, strong arms tightening around me and a low growl shaking his chest. "Why would you say that?"

I shrugged, inhaling a deep breath of his pine and sandalwood scent. "Weird dream, probably. Why are we on the roof?"

"We're almost surrounded," he replied, still growling. "Look."

I lifted my head off his shoulder and sucked in a sharp breath at the wall of opaque white fog surrounding the city limits, the tallest tips of the trees all-but hidden. "Fuck."

"Not a terrible suggestion," he drawled. "What else are we going to do to pass the time until we die? Get your clothes off then, Zaba."

I punched his shoulder, still staring at the Haar, wondering if I could convince it—him—to leave us undisturbed. "He's probably trying to get to you, Kier. The Haar is part of you."

"That *thing* is not me," he snarled, sharp fangs bared.

"Sure, buddy," I agreed sarcastically. "It's just your grief come to life, but definitely not a part of you."

He was quiet for a moment, tracing patterns on my back as we watched the fog. "I didn't mean to do this."

"I know," I agreed, putting my back to the city and the Haar, and looking at my husband. I startled at the shadows under his eyes, the tiredness cut into his face, his beard thicker than before. He looked worn down.

"I don't know how to undo it, but if you come home, Zaba—"

"I can't come home," I replied automatically, and then realised all at once this was *a dream*. I was exiled, Kier hated me, and this was all a pretty delusion.

But when he pressed a kiss to my forehead, his lips lingering, I decided I didn't care that this was fake.

"If you come home, I'll try things your way. Instead of attacking the Haar or bribing it with silversweet, I'll try to —to take it back. Inside me."

I let out a rough sigh, reaching up to trace his beard. "If you couldn't handle your grief before, it's so much stronger now. The Haar is powerful, Kier—"

"I know, but it doesn't matter what happens to me as long as—"

"Enough self-sacrificing shit," I snapped, making him smile.

"Fuck, I miss you," he exhaled, sinking his hands into my thick hair and bringing me closer for a long, tender kiss that bruised my already aching soul.

"I miss you, too," I whispered, my eyes fluttering. "Bastard."

"Come home," he entreated again. "Please, Zaba."

I groaned, letting my head fall on his shoulder and luxuriating in the strength and warmth of him. "The only downside of that great plan is outside my dreams, you want me dead. And all your guards have orders to murder me on sight."

"I reversed the exile within a week," he disagreed, his hands sliding down my back, fitting me closer to him. "You'll be welcomed, not murdered."

"Sure, dream Kier," I agreed, letting myself believe that for one delusional minute. "That'd be nice."

"If you come home, I can make good on all those promises," he murmured, laying a kiss in my hair.

"To mutilate me like you did my sister?"

He flinched. Good. "I didn't mean anything I said that day."

"You did," I laughed bitterly. "And that's fine, I tried to kill you—"

"You know I don't care about that. When the betrayal wore off, I found it actually hot to wake up with your knife to my throat. Let's recreate it."

"I was going to *murder* you," I hissed. "For real. I wasn't fucking around Kier, I meant it."

"It was still hot," he insisted. "And you couldn't have done it, anyway. I'm your mate."

"Thought you'd renounced me," I muttered, tempted to sink my teeth into his throat to claim him all over again. His neck was right there in front of my teeth, after all.

"I told you, when I got over the betrayal, I realised I'd made a mistake. Several, actually. I tried to find you, Zaba. I searched every city, town, and village we'd been to, but you'd vanished. I even went to—to your city in the human lands, but no one had seen you in months."

"You went to Seagrave?" I demanded, rearing back to stare at him and belatedly wondering why I was taking anything in this dream seriously.

"I did. You have a very impressive reputation by the way, Cutlass Lass."

I groaned. "I used a cutlass one time. One time! And now I'm stuck with that name for life."

That was port towns and sailors for you; always had to give someone a nickname, and once you were given one, it was for life. We might have been bastards, criminals, and whores in Seagrave's dark underbelly, but we were sailors and sons of sailors and granddaughters of sailors. So I was forevermore the Cutlass Lass of Seagrave Port.

And didn't that just prove this was all an elaborate dream? No way would the real Kier ever go to Seagrave. The bastard was too proud, too stubborn, too stuck in his hatred of humans.

"I was talking about my other promises," he murmured, stroking my back with his knuckles, his sapphire eyes dark as he gazed at me.

"Oh, those," I replied casually, flexing my hand where it rested on his chest, his body warm through the thin silk of his tunic. "I hadn't given them much thought."

Liar. His carnal promises were all I'd thought about at night in my tent when I struggled to sleep. Some nights I imagined his arms around me, like the rare night we'd spent in the same bed. It helped me sleep. Most nights I needed a little something extra, and dove into my fantasies. An orgasm or two always knocked me out.

Kier's chuckle worked through my body, stroking every sense. "I don't believe you."

"That's your problem, prince. Always thinking too

highly of yourself. Your promises just didn't make an impact on me."

His lips found my jaw, sucking a vicious mark onto my skin. I made a token effort to push him off, but when he growled, the sound purely possessive, a shiver swept my body and I groaned. It felt so damn good when his lips travelled down my neck, lingering on the places that made my breath catch.

When he drew back, I was languid and throbbing.

"No," he agreed, running his thumb over my bottom lip, pulling it from between my teeth. "Not much of an impact at all."

Smug fucker. I sank my fingers into Kier's long dark hair and hauled him to my mouth for a rough, heated kiss. But pain arrowed through my cheek before I could really sink into the kiss, and I jerked back.

"What is it?" he growled, gathering me close, his whole body rumbling with warning.

"I think ... someone slapped me," I breathed, reaching up to touch my skin where I felt warm.

"I'll end them," he seethed, his arms trembling around me. "I'll eat their heart and tear the skin from their body, piece by excruciating piece."

"What is it with you goblins and eating hearts? That's nasty, Kier."

"It forbids them entry to the Mother's afterrealm," he rumbled, his arms tightening around me when I flinched again, my face flaring with hot pain.

I held onto Kier, but he felt strangely insubstantial against me, more like a ghost than a man.

"I'm waking up," I realised. "Typical. Just when my dream was getting good."

"Zaba," Kier breathed urgently, taking my face between

his hands. "Kill them all, find out where you are, then fall asleep. Tell me where to find you."

"Sure, dream Kier," I agreed, but the rooftop and the Haar-wreathed city was already falling away.

"Come home," he ordered.

"Yeah, yeah," I muttered—and came awake with a vicious curse, trying to kick my legs in front of me and failing.

I'd been tied to a chair.

Of course I had.

# 12

"Were the slaps really necessary?" a sweet female voice asked. "Couldn't we have waited for her to wake up naturally?"

"My thoughts exactly," I muttered, my voice rough from sleep or a result of the sleeproot. "One slap I can understand, but *two*? Now, you're just on a power trip."

I peeled my eyelids apart and squinted at—huh, this wasn't a basement or dungeon. It was a pretty nice bedroom. Two people stood in front of me, both human—a petite blonde woman with a flower-print dress that must have cost a fortune and a tall, stern-looking man in his thirties with a long, black ponytail, dark tan skin, remarkably clear brown eyes, and a style of clothing I'd never seen before. Parts of fabric wrapped around his waist, others folding over his shoulders—hiding a sword sheath if the hilt sticking above his shoulder was anything to go by.

"It's dangerous to stay unconscious for so long with that high dosage," the man told his small companion.

"Dangerous to dose someone in the first place," I

muttered, assessing the bedroom around us, or at least what I could see while tied to a chair.

A bed lay to my right, looking pretty comfy and inviting with pillows piled near the wooden headboard, and thick velvet curtains blocked out the light coming through a small window. The rest of the room was sparse, just a chest of drawers pushed against the pale blue wall and a few rugs thrown over the bare floorboards.

"Would you have come willingly?" the serious guy asked, assessing me as I did a similar sweep of him, his posture and bearing indicating a fighter.

"Nope," I replied with a smirk. "But you could have left me to live my life instead of kidnapping me. Unlike *you*, I wasn't harming anyone."

"You have magic," the woman blurted, her green eyes wide and colour high on her cheeks. She was older than me, but there was an air of innocence that made me instantly resentful. "But you're human. You can use it to help us."

"Help you murder people?" I drawled, my eyelids heavy over my eyes as I gave her *a look.* "See, I've been there and done that. I thought I might change my life around, rehabilitate you know? Try helping people for a change."

The man snorted. "Once a killer, always a killer."

"Speaking from experience?"

He gave me a crooked grin that took him from stern to downright scary. "Yes."

Shit. My heartbeat quickened.

"Good for you. But I think I'll pass, so if you could untie me and let me go, that'd be great."

He snorted.

The woman knelt in front of me, the expression on her

pretty face almost pleading. "With you on our side, we can *end* this. We can stop people dying."

"People will always die," I disagreed. "Humans are assholes, goblins are assholes; you can't stop people killing people."

"On this *scale,* we can," she insisted. "If humans win the war—"

"We'll get revenge in a few years by invading the goblin lands, and this whole mess will start over again," I finished for her.

Judging by her expression, she'd planned to say something different.

"Look, I'm not saying I disagree with your goals; no war would be great. It's just unrealistic."

"Unrealistic," a new voice repeated, deeper, rougher. I craned my neck and saw an older man leaning against the door jamb, watching me like a hawk. He was short but muscular, with jet black hair and bright silver eyes that gave me the unsettling sense of being prey. I didn't like it. Only Kier was allowed to look at me like that.

"And yet," he went on, stepping into the room and moving with the same amount of power and brute force as a cannonball, "you got married because a temporary ceasefire was promised. You married for *peace.*"

My heart slammed against my ribs. My mouth dried up. So these humans knew who I was, and knew who I'd married.

I had two options—lie through my teeth, or tell the truth.

*Fuck it.*

I gave the older man a sneering laugh. "I married for *murder,* not peace. Sure, the treaty was a nice knock-on effect, but I married that bastard to kill him."

The three humans exchanged a glance. If I wasn't mistaken, excitement gleamed in the fighter's brown eyes.

The muscular, older man came closer, watching me intently enough to make me want to squirm. Because I was a trained assassin—and figurehead; thanks Celandrine—I didn't move an inch, but it was uncomfortable staying so still.

"You want Prince Kier dead?" he asked in that rough voice.

I let my next laugh turn a little twisted. "He'd be dead right now if he hadn't woken up when I had my knife to his throat."

At their shocked look, I went on, telling nothing but the truth. "I wanted to kill him as soon as the ceremony was over, but he can only be killed one night a year."

The fighter nodded. "The goblin moon."

So they knew that much. They'd obviously given serious thought to killing Kier. I suppressed a growl, and secretly nourished my plan to murder every single one of these bastards. Just as soon as they let me free—and I found out what their plan for Kier was.

Maybe I could return to Lazankh with a boon: information on an assassination attempt. *Come home,* dream Kier had said, and I wanted to.

I just knew I was returning to hatred and rage, not love and longing.

Still, I'd stay here and play these fuckers.

"Exactly," I agreed, looking from the small blonde to the long-haired warrior to the bulky older man who seemed to be in charge. Not that I'd make any assumptions about leading based on age. For all I knew, the petite woman was pulling their strings. Was she the mysterious *she?*

No, the man in Verna said she was a goblin, and this woman was too small to be a goblin in human form. Still, I kept an eye on her. On all of them.

"So I waited for the goblin moon and tried to slit his throat, but he woke up before I could end him." I let all my emotions shake my voice with fury, let them see the murderous hate on my face. The only thing I hid was my love.

"Why?" the woman asked, her voice softer than before. "Why marry him and ... and have to spend time with him and—how did you endure it?"

I rubbed my bound wrists together, clenching my jaw at the ache in my shoulder. Motherfucker, it was going to hurt when I got free.

"He killed my sister. He deserves to die." I looked them all dead in the eye, letting the assassin out to play, letting them see the vicious edges I hid from most people. "I *will* kill him. I don't care if it's the last thing I ever do, Prince Kier is fucking *dead.*"

The short wall of muscle smiled, so I'd said something right. The fighter wore a contemplative expression, his attention inward. But the woman leaned forward and squeezed my shoulder. It was less sympathetic because I was still tied to the chair.

"You got closer than we ever did," the older man said, still smiling. "That's impressive."

I shrugged, the move somewhat stunted by *being tied to a fucking chair.* "He never expected his harmless little wife to stab him. It won't work again; he'll be expecting me to come with knives."

"You'd be an effective distraction," he mused. "While we bring enough firepower to take him out."

I scoffed. "I lived with him for months. Nothing can kill him. Nothing."

"That's not strictly true," the long-haired fighter murmured, his eyes focusing again. "There's a way, but most refuse to consider it because the cost of using it is too high."

"Does it involve your fancy-looking sword?" I asked, testing the tension of the rope around my wrists. There wasn't a lot of give; these bastards were professional, I'd give them that.

"Best not to tell her details until she's proven herself," Mr. Muscle interrupted. I did *not* like the sound of proving myself. Not a single bit. "You're more useful to our cause than I realised," he told me, peering at me like he could see inside me.

"You've forgotten that I have zero interest in your little crusade," I said flatly, almost choking on the fanatic violence in the small bedroom.

"And travelling with goblin actors is a better future?" he replied archly.

"At least they don't want to use me—and don't deny you do. There's already been talk of using my magic for 'the cause.' And now you're going to use me as a distraction while you kill the prince? What if I have my own plan?"

"Do you?" the woman asked, watching me with open curiosity.

"Yes," I replied firmly. "And you're in the way of it. That troupe of actors is due back in Lazankh in a few weeks; I'll use them as cover to return to the castle and finish the job I started."

"How?" the fighter asked, heavy on doubt. "You failed the last time."

"He caught me off guard; I never expected him to wake up. This time I won't make the mistake of waiting for him to sleep. A knife through his skull should do the job nicely, what do you think?"

"Depends on the knife," he murmured.

Well, that was telling. They thought Kier could be killed by a specific blade?

"Together," the woman breathed, catching my gaze, "we can finish him, and end his cruel reign once and for all."

Cruel? Kier? As if. He was a bastard, but he loved his people. And cruel to humans? The only time he'd ever hurt a human was when—when *they* killed his baby sister first.

"What about the rest of them?" I asked, like I was considering joining them. "The other princes are said to *eat* humans. We could kill one and end up with two far, far worse."

"The others are in hiding," Mr Muscle murmured. "We'd need to find them first; but Kier is right in the open, not bothering to hide his whereabouts."

I raised an eyebrow. "And the queen *here*? Word has it she's even more of a monster than the Bluescale king." He was just lazy, useless, and neglectful. The Greenheart queen probably ate people's internal organs.

The three of them exchanged a significant look.

"She's not an issue," he said eventually, after a pregnant pause. "At least as far as Bluescale is concerned."

"No shit," I laughed. "You take out her enemies and she can expand her kingdom into the rest of the goblin lands. *Then* she'll kill us humans when we've outlived our purpose."

Another look. They didn't disagree with me. The

blonde opened her mouth to say something, but nothing came out. Oh, goody, these rebels were compelled like the three I killed.

They better not expect me to undergo similar treatment. No fucking way.

"First things first, Kier needs to die," the fighter said forcefully. "With him gone, the Bluescale goblins will weaken, and then we can find the princes and deal with the queen here."

"You've got it all thought out," I remarked, pulling at the ropes again. "Good for you. You're on your own with the queen and the other princes, but Kier's death is personal to me. So if there's a better chance of that bastard dying with us working together, then fine."

"You won't help us kill the rest of the goblins?" the woman asked, a furrow between her brows.

"I came here to kill one, and only one. Then I'm going home."

By the look the men exchanged, they planned to brainwash me into joining their little murder cult. Let them try.

"So," I asked, "are we temporary allies?"

Mr. Muscle nodded, and gestured at the fighter, the ropes around my wrists suddenly cut. I hissed as I relaxed my shoulders from their strained position, bringing my hands around to rub my wrists.

"Next time you're trying to get someone on side, don't tie them up," I grumbled. "It hurts like a bitch."

"Noted," the fighter muttered. "How do you have magic?"

I glanced down and forced my throat to bob. Made my hands shake. "That's none of your business."

"You're working with us now," the older man argued. "It is our business."

"Farrang," the blonde sighed. "Be kind. Can't you see she's traumatised?"

Traumatised by how predictable this conversation was.

Mr. Muscle, or *Farrang,* pressed his mouth into a thin line and ground out. "I'm sorry, Zabaletta."

"Just Letta, thanks," I corrected, rubbing a particularly sore spot in my wrist.

"It would help us if we understood the source of your power. Then we could replicate it, and better our chances of killing Prince Kier."

Not unless they discovered their own fated mates among the goblins, but I wasn't about to confess to *that* when I wanted them to think I was still Team Murder Kier.

"He forced it into me," I muttered, curling my hands into fists. "I don't remember specifics, just teeth and claws, and blood in my throat. I don't want to think about it. Satisfied?"

"For now," Farrang sighed. "But I want to know how he did it."

"Why?" I challenged, looking him in the eye as the blonde —I really needed to learn her name—untied my ankles from the chair. "Have you got a goblin friend lined up to help? I hate to break it to you, but humans can't give power to each other."

"Leave that to me," he replied mysteriously. Worryingly. "Focus on proving that your loyalty is to humans and not goblins."

I gave him a dark look. "My loyalty is to everyone who isn't an asshole and anyone who doesn't stand in my way."

"We'll see," he said ominously and ducked out of the room. "I'll expect you in the basement in an hour."

"For *what?*" I demanded, testing my freedom by standing. Holy shit, I could stand. The world was full of miracles.

"Your test," he replied from the hallway.

I blew out a breath, searching for my knives and coming up empty. "Alright, which of you fuckers robbed me?"

"Me," the fighter replied with a scowl. "Planning to stab anyone?"

"They're my comfort blanket. And no offence, but you bastards almost set me on fire once this week, *plus* you knocked me out and kidnapped me. You're not exactly number one on my most trusted list."

"You're safe here," the woman said giving me an understanding smile. "I know what it's like when you have to pretend to like goblins just to survive. But you're among your own kind now. Everything will be okay."

Oh, goody, she was *that* kind of person.

"Thanks," I croaked, clearing my throat. I could have a part on any stage; my acting skills were unrivalled.

When I looked at the fighter, he had an annoying smirk on his dark gold face. Okay, so maybe my skills had grown rusty these few months. Man, I missed my troupe and it had only been a few hours. It was weird not to hear Jakoda barking at everyone and Aerona whinging about putting up tents and Zaugustus—

Zaugustus was dead. Killed by these bastards, and their puppet master. I couldn't forget that.

First, I needed to find out their plan to kill Kier. Second, I wanted the names of everyone in charge, because no way was Farrang top dog. *Then* I'd raze them all in revenge for my friend—and for leading Natasya to her death.

"At least you've moved on from your harrowing time at the castle," the blonde said gently, reaching out to squeeze my hand. "You've found love again."

"Uh..." Had I? When did that happen?

She laughed, ducking her head before she leaned close to whisper, "You have marks on your neck and jaw; I can lend you a scarf if you want to conceal them."

For a moment, I couldn't hide my horror. I was forced to graciously accept her offer of a scarf just to cover my slip.

There were marks on my throat. And my jaw.

The places Kier's mouth had been in my dreams.

Ruthless. Fucking. Gods.

The dreams were real.

# 13

*J*iada—the sweet woman—and Zhin—stern fighter dick—left me in my shiny, new bedroom to prepare for my *test*. Whatever that test even was.

The second they were gone, I paced to the window, to the bed, and back again, halfway to a mental breakdown.

"Holy shit," I hissed under my breath, my hands in my hair, pulling tight. "Holy fucking *shit*. He marked—but that means—he said—"

I could hardly breathe. I suddenly needed to remember every single word Kier said in those dreams, but Zhin's double slap had knocked the memories out of my head.

He'd told me to come home. Repeatedly. And he—he fucking *kissed* me. Hell, in the dream before that, he went down on me. And it was *spectacular*.

I pulled at the roots of my hair. What if I was overreacting and they were just insect bites? Kier might still hate me and want me nowhere near; I shouldn't get my hopes up.

I dragged drawers open, searching their contents—clothes, towels, spare bed sheets—for a mirror and coming up empty. *Improvisation, it is.* I leaned over to the window and tilted my head until I could make out the ghost of my reflection.

Oof, I looked rough. My hair was in a ratted braid, there were bags under my eyes, and I looked ten years older than I had the last time I saw myself. There were also two red ovals on my neck, and one on the edge of my jaw.

*Son of a bitch.* Those weren't bug bites. That was the shape of Kier's mouth imprinted on my skin.

He couldn't have told me, once, during those dreams that *they were real* and he was actually there, not just a figment of my damned imagination?

I was going to kill him.

But first I had to stop these humans killing him. And survive whatever test of loyalty they'd set for me.

I searched the room top to bottom for a weapon and came up empty. Looked like I was going into this test of loyalty with only my hands—and my magic—to defend myself. Wait, why hadn't they taken my ring from me? Unless they didn't realise it was what gave me power...?

I tucked my necklace under my shirt and pressed my palm over the imprint. Kier wanted me to come home. The dreams were real.

Holy fucking gods.

I was still bewildered when Zhin came to collect me for the test, surprising me by handing me a plate with half a sandwich on it.

"Thanks," I said warily. "What did you drug me with this time? Hemlock?"

"Lettuce," he replied flatly. "Eat. I won't have Jiada complain we're starving you."

"Why do you care what Jiada says?" I muttered, pulling the sandwich apart to inspect it and beginning to eat it as he led me down a perfectly ordinary hallway. Strange place for rebels, but I wasn't complaining about having carpet or lighting.

"She's my wife," Zhin replied, snatching the plate as soon as I was done with my sandwich. Like he thought I would use it as a weapon. I would.

"Well, opposites attract," I murmured. "Anything you can tell me about this test?"

I warily followed him down a staircase, eyeing the family photos on the walls. None of my captors/allies were in the photos, which explained why the place was so nice. They'd broken in.

"No," Zhin grunted.

"Great. Thanks for your help."

My optimism for this whole thing plummeted even further when he opened a door at the bottom of the steps and I remembered Farrang saying *basement*.

I mentally prepared myself for torture devices and tested my body for soreness. My shoulders ached, but I could put up a fight if I needed. They could torture me all they wanted; if it got me information about their plan to kill Kier, I didn't give a shit.

Ugh, I really loved him. This was such an issue for me.

I flexed my hands as we reached the bottom of the dim staircase, following Zhin's straight back into a low-ceilinged basement made of bare stone. At the far end of the room, a woman hung from chains, her head dipped.

My heart skipped.

No.

Farrang turned at the sound of our footsteps, a hard expression on his face and blood on his knuckles. Rage began to pound in my chest, slow but powerful. When it built, it would be lethal.

"Prove you're on our side—the *right* side," Farrang ordered me. "Kill her."

I didn't need the woman to lift her head. I knew those messy black curls, knew her clawed blue hands and the voluminous layers of clothes.

Jakoda. They wanted me to kill Jakoda.

## 14

Obviously, I wasn't going to kill my friend, but I needed to stay with these rebels until I knew their plans. Not only for Kier, but—his people. Our people. These bastards could be planning any number of fires, explosions, and mass murders—they'd proven they had zero scruples about killing innocents, goblin *or* human. Bluescale had enough to contend with; we didn't need another threat on top of the Haar.

We. That word echoed, especially as I took slow, measured steps through the basement towards Jakoda.

"Who is she?" I asked, as if I didn't know her instantly.

"The leader of the troupe," Farrang replied, glaring at Jakoda like she'd personally insulted him. She probably had; if they had me in chains, I'd have done the same.

"Ohhh," I breathed with understanding, squinting at her. "I see it now. And you want me to kill her because...? You just picked her at random?"

"I'm an opportunist," Farrang replied smoothly, that scary little smile of his reappearing. "We caught her and you together; why go to the trouble of finding another task for you when she's right here?"

I shrugged. "Fair enough. Never really liked her anyway."

Jakoda lifted her head to glare at me; I glared right back.

*You really think I'm going to kill you, bitch?*

Zhin came forward, moving silently enough to unnerve me, and handed me a small knife. I glanced from the knife to his face.

"You wouldn't let me keep a plate, but you'll arm me with a knife? Makes sense." I snorted. "And I don't need a knife; I have magic, remember?" I turned to Farrang. "I'm guessing you want to see what it can do?"

He tilted his head, considering. "Can you use it in the same way goblins do?"

"No idea," I replied flippantly, closing the distance between me and Jakoda and trying not to flinch at the mess they'd made of her face. "But I have my own signature style."

I tugged my ring out from under my shirt and closed my fingers around it.

"What are you doing?" Farrang demanded in his coarse voice, watching me like a vulture eyeing scraps.

"Using my magic," I replied flatly, heavily implying *you fool.* "My cruel husband bound my blood to this ring; it's how I do *this.*"

I hoped he didn't hear the way my tongue lovingly formed the word *husband,* and focused instead on Valour as she leapt from the room and snarled, teeth bared, at Farrang and Zhin.

*Growl at Jakoda too, you moron,* I ordered her. *We're trying to be subtle here.*

She spun and growled louder, impressively, at my friend. *Better.*

Jakoda paled, her green skin sickly and wan. I wanted to give her another significant look, but I didn't dare risk it.

"If I do this," I said to Farrang across the cold basement, "I've proven myself to you?"

He nodded, bulky arms crossing over his chest. "I'll know you side with humans, not goblins."

*Sure, buddy.*

*Murder: the world's biggest sign of being trustworthy.*

I turned back to Jakoda and made sure she met my gaze before I grinned. "Then let's play."

Understanding flickered through her green eyes at the choice of words—play like *players*—and she quickly masked her relief.

"Do your worst, traitor," she croaked.

"Oh, believe me," I replied, ordering Valour to prowl closer, her fangs bared. "I will."

Valour launched at Jakoda, and closed her jaws around my friend's leg. There was a tiny, barely noticeable pause between teeth supposedly sinking in and Jakoda's howl of pain, but stubbornness could easily explain it. I bet it had taken her a while to scream when they beat her before I was brought in.

"Ruthless gods," Zhin murmured when Valour released Jakoda's leg and went for her throat. My friend was already covered in blood, so it looked convincing enough when she howled, a perfect sound of pain and rage.

Oh, she was good.

*Swipe her for real, somewhere non-lethal,* I told Valour, forcing my grin to stay in place even as Jakoda cried out for real. But she met my eyes with fury and I saw the understanding and forgiveness underneath.

"How do you want her killed?" I asked Farrang, glancing at him over my shoulder.

"Stomach wound," he replied without any contemplation. "Let her die slowly."

I shrugged and nodded at Valour, my jaguar pretending to sink her fangs into Jakoda's stomach. Instead, she lapped at an existing wound, helping my friend heal. Not that Jakoda's guttural roar suggested she was healing. I was impressed.

I raised an eyebrow at Farrang. Happy?

"Good," he grunted, his eyes pouring down Jakoda's body, gloating at all the blood, at her twisted expression of pain. "Now, the ring."

"The what?"

He held out his hand. Valour bared her teeth.

"Knock it off," I warned her.

*Later,* I promised secretly.

She plopped onto her haunches by my feet and stopped snarling, but she didn't hide how little she liked Farrang.

"Why do you need my ring?" I asked warily, my fingers still wrapped around it. "You're asking me to be helpless around people I just met and don't yet trust. People who kidnapped me, in case you've forgotten. This—" I waved a hand at Jakoda's moaning form. "Proved my loyalty, but what about *yours?*"

"I'll tell you our plan for Kier," he replied, holding my gaze with his beady eyes. "But I need the ring, Zabaletta."

"Just Letta," I insisted, weighing my options. But if this got him to confess all his nefarious plans, it would be worth it.

"Here," I growled, giving Valour a look to return to the ring. She made her displeasure known, but jumped back inside the jewellery, and I handed it over with extreme difficulty.

The second it was in his hands, I knew I'd fucked up. A queasy feeling twisted my stomach, and I had to physically fight the compulsion to snatch it back.

But Farrang closed his meaty hand around my chain and ring, and said, "I'll give it back when we leave for Lazankh."

"And what about the rest of your little jobs?" I asked wryly. "Like burning the theatre in Verna? Any more surprise arson parties planned?"

He and Zhin glanced at each other.

"Not that we know of," Farrang replied finally, a tad raspier.

"Just don't expect me to get involved," I warned them, giving Jakoda a sneering look—checking she was okay—before I headed for the stairs. "I only agreed to kill Kier, remember?"

"You've made that clear," Zhin remarked, clearly disapproving. Aww, did he not like me refusing to needlessly murder people? So sad.

"Well?" I asked with my foot on the first step. "Are we going to plan the prince's murder, or what?"

I was glad when they followed me up into the main house, leaving Jakoda alone. Not checking she was really, truly dying.

That had gone according to my hasty plan, at least. But losing my ring made me weak and sickly, and I didn't know how to get it back.

# 15

*I* rolled over in bed, clutching my stomach as sickness roiled, an unwelcome tightness in my chest refusing to let me sleep. I needed to *sleep*, dammit. I wanted to know if the dreams were real, or if I was going mad with delirium and it wasn't actually Kier in those dreams with me. And I wanted to know where the rest of my troupe were; they could be strung up in a different basement for all I knew. They could be dead.

When I rolled over again, and this time threw up over the side of the bed, I decided enough was enough. I needed my damn ring back. I needed Valour, and my magic. It was part of me, and clearly a part I couldn't live without.

Avoiding the pool of vomit, I climbed out of bed and pulled my boots and coat on. I wasn't armed, and I was without magic, but I still had my training and no one could take that from me. Plus, the boots were heavy; great for kicking in skulls.

They made it harder to creep out of the room without being heard, but they were well worth the sacrifice.

No one sat outside the door guarding me, which was an oversight. Also, unexpected. I'd thought Zhin would be here, suspicious to the end, but maybe Jiada had insisted he stay with her. Wives got privileges after all. I was looking forward to cashing in my own. If my dreams were actually real, if Kier actually *did* forgive me and want me home.

We'd find out soon enough.

I crept down the hallway, my eyes on the door to Farrang's office at the end. I knew my necklace was locked in the top drawer of his desk; I'd watched him squirrel it away before he told me all his wicked plans.

The rebels had a dagger said to have killed the current Bluescale king's father, and while I didn't know where to find it because it was with their leader—whoever he was —I *had* learned Farrang wasn't the top dog. He and three others answered to a big bad boss, who in turn answered to the mysterious *she*. They'd all been compelled, though he hadn't told me that part. It was obvious.

The crux of their plan revolved around waiting for the Haar to lure Kier out of Lazankh, and taking out all his guards—killable since they weren't royals—while they were occupied with the fog. Then when Kier was vulnerable and alone, they'd stab him, drain his strength, and hack off his head.

I'd suggested they just slit his throat but the rebels were very attached to the hacking plan. I was surprised they didn't want to cut out his heart and eat it. Not that they could have his heart. That was mine, and I was very possessive of it.

I was also getting dangerously attached to the idea of Kier wanting me, and it wasn't even confirmed.

I made my steps even lighter as I passed the other two

bedrooms on this floor—and smirked at the sound of bedposts knocking into a wall. That explained why Zhin wasn't guarding me. I heard Jiada swear sharply and made an impressed face. Sounded like Zhin knew what he was doing. Good for him.

At least they were busy, and the sound of their bed hitting the wall covered up my last few steps to Farrang's office. I didn't have any lock picks, but I'd found a pair of hat pins in the drawers in the bedroom, so it only took me a minute to get the door unlocked.

I opened it carefully, making sure it didn't creak, and slipped inside, swiftly shutting it behind me. I couldn't afford to light the lamp and risk someone noticing I was in here, but I crossed the messy office to the small window above the desk and cracked the curtains open, letting in a faint glow of moonlight.

When I faced the room again, my attention snagged on the wall opposite, and I had to resist the urge to let out a low whistle. There was a huge, hand-drawn diagram of a building, so intricate and detailed that I couldn't imagine how long it must have taken to create.

The curved edges of towers caught my attention, and my eyes narrowed as I counted them.

"Shit," I breathed, and crept closer, scanning the floor plan until I found the kitchens, then from there followed it up to the throne room, then deeper in the castle to the courtyard. This was my damn castle. Why did the rebels need a floorplan when their plan relied on luring Kier *out*?

And why hide this earlier? I'd have remembered if this map was here when I was here earlier with Farrang.

There were notes scrawled in pencil beside the inky strokes of walls and doorways; I clenched my teeth as I read each and every one, aware I was taking too long but refusing to stop until I knew everything.

Luring Kier out of Lazankh, my ass! Why were three doorways marked *potential entrance* and why was the secret doorway behind the grubby door where Calanthe had taken me to the market circled? ESCAPE ROUTE was written in brutal capitals beside it.

"Lying bastards," I whispered in a hiss, not sure why I was surprised. They were humans; we lied as easily as breathing. The rebels' plan was laid out in these schematics, as clear as water. They'd hit the castle from three angles, one group going right for the guards' rooms and removing that complication while another would hit the throne room from the main entrance and another snuck in from the back door. How the hell did they know about the back door?

"We have a mole," I realised, rage mounting.

I grabbed the pins from the corners of the map, tucking them into my pocket and swearing to stab them into Farrang's eyeballs. Maybe I'd save one for the eyes of whoever had betrayed Kier in his own damn castle. Not only had someone drawn this accurately, but they'd told the rebels how to get in, get to Kier, and get out again. Who knew what else they'd told them?

I needed space to examine this more clearly, and here was definitely not the time. I rolled up the floorplan and stuck it under my arm while I rounded the desk, trying the top drawer. Locked. Well, a girl could try.

I still had my hat pins, so I knelt and tested the lock, the tumblers on this drawer far more stubborn than the door.

"Son of a bitch," I grunted, losing my grip on the

tumbler for the third time. Who had a lock this sophisticated on a damn drawer?

"People with something to hide," I muttered, my tongue sticking out as I tried another angle and—yes! The lock clicked, and I wasted no time in tearing the drawer open, forgetting to be quiet.

My necklace sat atop a leather-bound journal, with other rings, brooches, and pendants scattered around it. Huh. Looked like Farrang collected magical objects. I slid my necklace over my head, the queasy sickness that coated my stomach like oil instantly beginning to soothe. My dagger was gone, though. Bastard probably pocketed it.

The other pieces of jewellery caught my attention. Were they Farrang's or had he stolen these, too? Did he rob the bodies of his victims?

I scooped all the pieces up in my hand and slid them into the pocket of my jacket, flicking through the journal, too.

*I tried to run, but I didn't get further than the front step before her magic dug its claws into me. Pain made me useless, and it didn't stop until I crawled back inside the house and admitted, aloud, that I couldn't run, that I wouldn't try again. I could only leave the house today because she gave us orders to hunt the Bluescale and force them out of the kingdom. I don't know how she'll react to us abducting the old goblin, or finding the traitor princess. I dread her response when she finally finds out.*

I blinked—and blinked again, absorbing this information. So the rebels were trapped in this house until their master called. And the mysterious *she* didn't know they'd brought me on board yet.

I tapped my fingernails against two incredibly rude words, and glanced up when the door creaked open.

It was too late to hide, and I was pissed off, so I only gave Farrang an arch look and asked, "Traitor princess? That's not very nice. And I'd *just* decided to be your friend."

The big man assessed me with eerie silver eyes, spying his open drawer and the rolled up paper under my arm. "What do you think you're doing, Zabaletta?"

"I'm starting to think you use my full name just to piss me off now," I muttered, standing and tucking the journal into my pocket, too.

"What. Are you *doing?*" he repeated, his voice biting.

"What does it look like?" I huffed. "I'm stealing your shit. Honestly, though, I only came for my ring. I appreciate the offer of helping me kill the prince, but I'm not a team player. I'm doing this alone. Thanks for the plans of the castle, though. That's a handy little exit you've found."

Farrang closed the door, like he didn't want the others to hear this conversation. Or to witness whatever he planned to do to me. That made my life easier. I almost thanked him for it.

"You're not leaving," he growled, flexing his hands. Ohhh, was he going to strangle me? In that case, I knew exactly how I'd kill him.

I smiled, nice and slow. Let him see all the shit that was wrong with me, and my jagged, dysfunctional mind. "I'd like to see you try."

He fluttered his hands, and for a moment I thought I was seeing things as the back of his hand began to glow. But no, that was really magic, and under his skin, an emerald oval was brighter than the rest of his hand. Holy shit, was this how the woman was controlling them? She'd embedded gemstones in their body?

"You're, uh, glowing," I told him, in case he didn't know.

His grin suggested he did.

*Valour,* I barked, summoning her at the same moment Farrang slashed his hand through the air and threw a net of emerald green magic at me.

"How do you have magic?" I demanded, scrambling out of the path of the net and letting out a tiny breath when Valour roared into existence. She gnashed her jaws through his magic, sawing the magic apart.

Ha! I was more powerful than him. This was going to be fun.

"I was gifted it," he replied, assessing me for a weakness.

"Bullshit. I just read your diary; I know you're trapped in this house. Gifted? More like cursed."

"The magic is the only good thing to come out of our arrangement."

He thrust his palm flat towards me and I ducked on instinct, screeching when the desk slammed into my stomach, pinning me to the wall.

"The others will hear you," I pointed out, wheezing. Shutting the door was redundant with noise that loud.

"This whole office is surrounded by a bubble of magic. They won't hear your screams, Zabaletta."

Of course it was silenced. Fuck.

I heaved against the desk, but it was made of solid wood and it didn't budge. I gritted my teeth, the place where it had me pinned throbbing with a vicious new bruise.

"It takes a lot to make me scream," I grunted, giving

Valour a silent command, "and I highly doubt you're man enough, Farrang."

I braced my boot against one of the feet of the desk and shoved, buying myself a centimetre. Judging by Farrang's low grunt, Valour had leapt at him. The lack of a crash said she'd failed to knock him over, though. Annoying.

I kicked the desk again, getting an inch of space. I dug my hand into my pocket, finding the other jewellery I'd stolen. I'd never used anything other than my ring but I didn't have time for a learning curve. Remembering what Cherish had taught me these few months, I picked a ring and jammed my finger through it. The metal was too big for my finger, but the second it connected with my skin, I felt my magic flare. Felt Valour soak up the extra strength.

This time Farrang roared, and I managed to shove the desk away and get back to my feet. I'd earned a throbbing rib in the process, but I could handle it.

"Why lie about your plan to kill Kier?" I asked, sliding over the desk and getting a sick satisfaction from watching all his books and documents slide to the floor. "Why not tell me you're going to break into the castle? I *lived* there; I could have helped."

"Hedging my bets," he grunted, grappling with Valour's open jaws. She was trying to rip out his throat, growling deep in her own. *That's my girl.* Her growl thrummed lower. A purr? "Didn't trust you."

"It's mutual," I told him, wincing at a slash of pain through my middle. "Probably because you stole my only source of magic. Fun fact; being without it makes me violently sick. I left a puddle of vomit in the bedroom; sorry about that, buddy."

I wasn't. He deserved it for kidnapping me.

*Kill him,* I ordered Valour.

Her blue body rumbled with an excited noise and she tore away from Farrang, breaking their stalemate before she went for his thigh and gnashed her fangs deep. Oof, that looked painful. Blood welled, dragging a low snarl of pain from Farrang.

"Your sister would be ashamed of you," the bastard said without prompting, kicking Valour's chest. She only skidded back a step, recovering fast and slashing her claws through his thigh, widening the wound.

"Good," I replied shortly. "The feeling is mutual. I take it you're the one who encouraged her to steal the stone?"

A muscle throbbed in Farrang's forehead as he stared at me, only Valour between us. I kept an eye on his glowing hand, waiting for his next strike. Although, men like him liked to play with their victims; I'd met enough of them to know he was going to drag this out as long as he could.

"She was one of my best rebels," he replied, sighing like he was saddened she was dead. I didn't buy it.

"Until she got killed working for you," I pointed out, sensing Valour winding up for another assault as I panted for breath. "Killing a little kid will do that to you. You know, I'd like to think your mission to kill Kier is out of revenge for Natasya's death, but I'm not convinced you have enough compassion for that. No offence."

Farrang laughed, the sound scornful. "She was killed because of that *monster,* not us."

"Disagree," I replied, and jerked forward to distract him while Valour dove for his side, her sharp teeth aiming for the vulnerable fleshy bit.

I was so focused on the emerald magic buried in his hand that I took my eye off his other one, and never saw him draw a weapon. I only realised he had a knife when it spun through the air and sank into my chest, too damn fast for me to avoid it.

*"Fuck!"* I howled, panicking. Had it pierced my lung? What side was my heart on? No, the other side.

I wanted to tear the knife out and throw it into his skull, but I wasn't stupid enough to do that. It needed to stay where it was until I was sure *what* it had cut.

"Valour," I growled. "End this."

"I don't believe you, you know?" he told me, a sneer still twisting his face. "You didn't take the castle plans so you can kill the prince alone. You just don't want us to kill him."

I shrugged and wished I hadn't when pain arrowed deeper. "Strangely enough, Kier has more honour in his little finger than all of you rebels put together. I might hate him, but I trust him not to put a knife in my back the second it's turned. Or my chest, I suppose," I murmured, glancing down at the hilt sticking out of my body.

I breathed faster, sharper. Pain spread ruthlessly, and this was no bruise I could still fight with. This would take me down; it was only a matter of when.

*Valour!* I ordered, but she seemed far weaker when she flew at Farrang, and it took me a moment to realise my wound had affected her, too.

It took her two attempts, but she finally got the bastard knocked to the floor. Emerald magic sputtered in his hand but died when I crossed the room, keeping him down with a boot on his chest while Valour ripped out his throat. She spat it on the rug. Lovely.

Panting, I knelt, mindful of his hands and any weapons they might grab—or magic they might summon —and I put my fingers to his throat.

No pulse. Thank fuck for that.

Valour whined, watching me get clumsily back to my feet. Her body was fainter, paler blue instead of the rich colour it usually was. If she was getting weaker, I was probably losing too much blood.

*Find a towel or bandage,* I told her. *And anything that looks antiseptic.*

Her ears flattened to her head and she made her displeasure known. I waved a weak hand.

*If we split up, we'll get out faster. I'll be fine; I'm going to get Jakoda from the basement, and then we're out of here.*

I put my second ring on my thumb so I didn't lose it and made sure the castle plans were secure under my arm as I stepped over Farrang's cooling body, scanned the office for anything else I might want to pilfer, and then ducked back into the hall.

What were the chances of us getting out of this house without me being stabbed again?

# 16

*othing to see here,* I thought as I moved quietly down the hall. *Just a girl with a knife sticking out of her chest, totally normal, move along.*

Jiada's bed was still slamming noisily into the wall as I passed. My eyebrows climbed up my forehead. It must have been thirty minutes, maybe more. *Damn, Zhin. Good man.*

Valour huffed, letting her disapproval known as she walked through the bathroom door—literally, phasing through the wood—and I headed for the staircase. I clutched the railing with clammy hands, going over the positives in my head so I didn't focus on the negatives.

One. I had a map marked with the rebel's plans to assassinate Kier. Even if I was crazy and he still hated me, this would at least buy me an audience with him.

Two. I had a journal that probably contained names of the other rebels, and maybe told me who the woman pulling all their strings was.

Three. I now had four extra items of power to help me channel more magic. That gave me five, and while I wasn't rivalling Hames's impressive jewellery collection any time soon, it was a big step up from a single ring.

I wavered three steps from the bottom of the stairs, pain hitting me in a rush. I fumbled for the railing and managed to stay upright through sheer will, cutting off a whimper in my throat.

"Four," I gasped, breathing slowly until I had a handle on the pain and wasn't about to face-plant the steps. "I have a new knife."

Sure, it was embedded in my body, but it was brand new and no one could take it from me.

Five. Backup was almost certainly on the way. I was surprised the house wasn't surrounded by white fog already.

I reached the bottom of the stairs and took a fortifying breath before I opened the door to the basement. I suppressed a groan at the darkness beckoning from downstairs. It was bad enough navigating these steps when I was pain-free, but with a stab wound and throbbing ribs?

"You're a strong, capable assassin," I breathed, psyching myself up as I took the first step and latched my hand around the cold metal railing. "Remember when Marc the Scythe caught you stealing wine from his cellar and beat the shit out of you? You got through that; you can endure this, too."

I wasn't sure if I blacked out or if it was just the darkness of the basement, but I barely processed anything until my foot met the solid floor at the bottom.

Jakoda still hung from the chains where I'd left her, looking dead to all intents and purposes. Panic that she was really, truly dead made my heart race, and I stumbled as fast as I could across the cold basement, grasping her shoulders.

"Rats," she croaked.

"Huh?" I searched for a weakness in the chains, wondering where the hell Valour was. She better have found a whole crate of bandages; I needed to take the knife out and put pressure on my wound.

"Rats," Jakoda grunted, her expression tight with rage. "Trap."

I swore viciously, glancing at the ground and finding it empty. But when a scratching sound came from behind me, I turned slowly. My breathing shattered.

Fifty rats made of emerald magic phased through the wall, piercing my ears with their cries as they ran right at us. No, at *me*.

# 17

$\mathcal{I}$ skittered away from the rats and pressed myself to the wall beside Jakoda so nothing could sneak up on me, frantically running through everything Cherish had taught me. Wielding two kinds of magic at the same time took practice and effort, and I'd barely practised at all. I'd grown lazy and complacent, dependent on Valour.

But there was an army of magical green rats racing for me, and either Farrang wasn't as dead as he seemed or this magic came from another source. Someone who might have felt him die and leave her network of magical slaves, and then sent her creatures to get revenge. I couldn't imagine how powerful someone would have to be to bring this many creatures to life, though. I struggled with just Valour.

As the glowing green rats raced at me, I took another breath, curled my fingers into a fist, and reached for my power.

The ring around my neck and the one on my hand both glowed pale blue, nowhere near as bright as usual.

Well, beggars couldn't be choosers. I'd have to make do with the scraps of power I had left, and hope my wound didn't drain me before I took out the rats. The room was a little bit blurry and swirly, not good signs.

I gave Valour a sharp order to come to the basement at the same time I grabbed more power and visualised a wall rising from the floor, blocking the rats from us.

It flickered to life, unsteady but undeniable, and my shoulders sagged as I turned to Jakoda, pulling at the links of her chains. With my rings glowing, I was able to get her out of them, but by the time the chains fell to the floor, I was drained and wavering on my feet.

*"Letta,"* she warned, her voice as raspy and thin as my own.

I turned with a groan. The rats had run straight through my wall like the bricks were cobwebs. Typical.

I waved a flimsy hand, dismantling the bricks. *Can you make me a mouser?* I asked my power. *Something powerful and fluffy, with big claws?*

I'd been picturing a *cat,* but the monster my magic coalesced was more of a lion with a thick ruff of fur around its head, vicious knives for claws, and glowing sapphire eyes. I wanted to pet her instantly.

She growled in the back of her throat before she dove into the crowd of rats, snapping powerful teeth down to snatch them up, shaking her head and—ohhhh, she growled because *she* was a *he.*

*Sorry, baby,* I apologised, *the pain's messing with my head.*

Where the hell was Valour and my bandages? *Get down here,* I barked, and flinched at the hellish crunch my new mouser let out as he chomped through rats.

Valour threw back a sense of impatience and frustration. That's what I got for sending a girl lacking opposable thumbs for first aid supplies.

"Fuck," I gasped when tiny, magical teeth sank into my ankle. I kicked the rat off with a pathetically weak motion, and slammed my boot down on its glowing body. Regret twinged in my chest for hurting the furry baby, but it was kill or be killed. Or whatever their master would do when she caught me. I knew being compelled would be a hundred times worse than being killed.

*Get all of them,* I barked at my mouser, my fingers clenching around my ring so hard, metal bit into my fingers. I hissed when the ground wobbled under me; I had to rest against the wall so I didn't fall over. Blood had soaked my clothes all the way to my waist. Not good.

"Open your eyes," Jakoda barked, kicking aside her chains and grabbing my face.

I groaned in complaint. I didn't even know when my eyelids had fallen shut.

"Where did you get this ring?" she demanded, noticing the new one on my hand.

"Office," I rasped, forcing my eyes open a flicker. "More in my pocket."

She plundered my coat pockets and found a brooch, a weak smile curving her lips as she clenched her fist around it and blue light blazed from her fingers.

I sometimes thought goblins' reliance on objects to channel their power limited them. But it was better than being burned alive by unchecked magic, I guessed. Still, if she hadn't needed a damn ring, she could have got herself out of the chains before I was ever stabbed.

I forced my eyes open even though they wanted to fall shut, and shock pulsed through my chest when Jakoda swept her hand out in a wide arc and the rats all *squealed* like they'd been electrocuted.

"Remind me ... never get on your ... bad side," I laughed weakly. And sluggishly added, "Don't hurt my baby."

"He's made of magic; he can't *be* hurt," she snapped, gritting her teeth as she sent another wave of pain at the glowing green rats.

Oh sure, *she* was lucid enough to realise my mouser's true gender.

The rats squealed when her magic touched them, but didn't stop coming at us, either supremely stubborn—which was relatable—or commanded by their master to fight to their deaths. I'd put my money on the latter. Not that I had any money. All mine burned when these bastards set my tent on fire.

"Get that one there," Jakoda barked at my mouser.

My eyes were slipping shut, so I didn't see what he did, or which rat she meant. *Yeah, what she said,* I told him.

"You're using too much magic at once," she berated someone, presumably me. "You're too weak for this, Letta."

I tried to wave my hand, but I barely twitched my finger. Ugh, this reminded me of when I got pricked by a needle covered in a paralysing drug during a robbery. I'd successfully stolen the ancient vase, but on my way out, the drug had hit my system and I tumbled down a flight of stone steps, breaking both the vase and several of my own bones.

I eyed the dark steps up to the main house, and told the ruthless gods I didn't want a repeat of that day.

A sudden roar filled my ears, as loud as a cannon.

"What ... hell ... noise?" I slurred, the blood loss draining me of strength and, apparently, speech.

"That's your cat purring," Jakoda replied in a huff, and followed it up with a vicious threat, hopefully at a rat and not my mouser.

Awww, did murder make him happy? "Me too, baby," I murmured, my tongue strangely numb.

"Five left," Jakoda told me or my cat, magic flashing through my closed eyelids, emerald and blue clashing.

I slit my eyes open when the purr grew louder. My mouser clamped his jaws around the last rat and shook his head until it dissolved, the magic returning to wherever it had come from. This puppet master controlling humans was an issue. Something told me she wouldn't forgive and forget us killing her rebels.

"Letta?" Jakoda barked, storming towards me. "Still with us?"

I made a groan of assent, and jumped when a solid weight pressed on my legs. If it wasn't for the wall, I'd have toppled over. The last thing I needed was a bruised backside to add to my list of injuries.

My mouser rubbed against my leg, a sign of love that was determined to knock my feet from under me.

"Good job, baby," I praised in a slur.

He purred louder, the sound like thunder. Weakly, I fluttered my fingers and gave him a silent order to return. He rubbed his head against me again and leapt into the ring, visible in my wavering sight as a stream of light.

"Let's get this damn knife out," Jakoda huffed, stomping closer to grab my shoulders when I nearly lost my battle with gravity.

"'S'mine," I complained.

"Yeah, yeah, you can keep it," she muttered.

I let my eyes finally flutter shut, but they flew open when she tore the knife out of me and pressed a clean tunic against the hole in my chest. I was touched that she'd parted with one of her many layers for me.

"We'll have to keep an eye on this for infection," she told me, her voice strange and echoey. "Are the others dead?"

"Leave them," I slurred. "Busy. Let's go."

Jakoda wrapped her arm around my back, and I slumped into her. The journey up the stairs took five times as long as the way down. I groaned when pain flared, but gritted my teeth and endured it.

"Gaia's tits!" Jakoda hissed when we finally reached the top. She almost dropped me when Valour came racing down the stairs with a bundle of cotton clamped in her jaws. "Don't go around creeping up on people! What've you got?"

Valour let out a warning growl when Jakoda tried to take the bundle. She made it very clear she'd only give it to me. I made it very clear I was about to pass out.

"Outside," I said, my tongue refusing to move the way I wanted. It came out as *ousssa*, which was sadly not a word.

Jakoda gripped me tighter and towed me towards the front door, and I kept my eyes open by sheer will, searching the ordinary residential street for a low-slung fog or creeping smoke.

My heart sank when I found it empty. Where was he? Hadn't he felt me get stabbed?

I didn't fight it when my eyes drifted shut, a tight pain spreading through my fractured mate bond.

"Gaia!" someone swore in a breathless hiss, and footsteps pounded the pavement towards us. "We were coming to break you out. What happened?"

Ryvan...?

"I'll carry her," Hames offered soberly.

I bit back a scream of pain when I was passed into a strong pair of arms, swung up against a cold chest. Why was he cold? Oh, that was *not* good. Was I feverish? It might already be too late to avoid infection.

*Give ... supplies,* I ordered Valour, losing my grip on consciousness. When I passed out, she'd disappear back into my ring.

"What's this?" Cherish asked, her voice low and worried. "Oh. Clever girl."

Valour let out a low, pleased sound and jumped back into my ring, filling my chest with warmth.

"Letta?" Ryvan asked, a soft prod meeting my arm.

"Missed ... the party," I slurred, and passed out in Hames's arms.

# 18

*I* woke up with my tongue stuck to the roof of my mouth and an awful funk coating my senses. I felt like I'd been asleep for millennia, my eyes scratchy and crusted, my body aching all over but especially at my shoulder.

I groaned, rolling over in bed—and grunting when my hip met the bare padding of a mat instead of a soft, comfortable mattress.

"Finally," Aerona growled, her low voice strangely soft. "You've been asleep for three days."

Three days, and not a single dream?

I hauled my eyes open, moving my least aching arm so I could scratch the sleep from my lashes and blink at my small, fierce friend.

"Hey, you," I croaked.

"You sound like death," she replied, her lips pressed thin, which was much more familiar than the softness. "Drink this."

She thrust a flask at me, and helped me sit up so I wouldn't choke on the liquid inside. Water. Disappointing

—I wanted something made from turnips that tasted foul but packed a wicked punch.

"Thanks," I said, my voice less rough. "You on babysitting duty?"

"I volunteered, actually," she retorted, heavy on the attitude. Her black hair was in its usual twin braids, but the shadows around her eyes made her look older than usual.

I lifted my arm and gave her a bossy look.

"What?" she demanded, crossing her arms over her thin chest.

"We're hugging."

"We are not!"

"Yes we are. Get in here."

"You're *injured,*" she muttered, but leaned over and lightly squeezed me. "Moron."

"Thanks for taking care of me," I murmured, patting her hair as a weight lifted from my chest. I'd been worried about the rest of my troupe the whole time I pretended to hate goblins for Farrang and co. "You're actually pretty sweet, Aerona. And don't worry," I added quickly, "I'll never repeat that again."

"You better not," she hissed, but squeezed me tighter before letting go. "I'll find you some food. You must be starving."

"No dumpling soup," I ordered, pulling myself from under the covers and assessing my body. Someone had changed me into clean clothes, and the dressing on my stab wound was both fresh and packed with something rank-smelling and dark green.

Aerona froze on the edge of the tent. Not my familiar tent with its water stains around the bottom, but a new one. I had no idea where it came from. I'd missed so much in the three days I was passed out, healing a damned knife wound.

"What have you got against dumpling soup?" Aerona demanded fiercely. "It's the best soup."

"It reminds me of my husband, and then I want to cry," I answered honestly.

Her eyes flew wide; her mouth dropped open. The expression made her look her age more than the pigtails ever did. "You have a *husband*? Since when?"

"Get me that food and gather everyone together," I replied tiredly. "I'll tell you all this secret at once. It's about time I confessed, anyway."

Aerona's eyes narrowed. "Confessed to what?"

I flapped my good hand. "Food. Now."

She pointed a threatening finger at me, but she was obviously still worried about my health because she didn't threaten me with a knife. "If you're secretly a nun, I'm gonna be so mad."

I barked a laugh. "Definitely not a nun. Although, I did know a very cool nun back in Seagrave. She helped us get shipments of stolen food to the needy. Drank me under the table a few times. I miss that nun."

Aerona gave me a very strange look but said nothing else before ducking under the tent flaps and crunching grass under her boots.

"Dickhead's awake," she announced, which was rude but expected. Name-calling was just one of Aerona's many colourful love languages.

I knelt, gritting my teeth against a groan, and glanced around the tent. Fresh clothes had been piled beside me and—more importantly—my new knife was with them, cleaned of blood and oiled until it shone. Hames must have cleaned it up; he was the only one who knew how to do it properly. Ryvan wouldn't know a clean dagger if it stabbed him in the ass. He thought wiping it on his pants made it as good as new.

I dressed and hunted down my knife sheath. When I buckled it around my waist and shoved my feet into boots, I felt more like myself. My shoulder throbbed, but dully, and I wasn't woozy with blood loss anymore. I probably had Hames's healing magic to thank for that.

"Thank the Mother," Cherish breathed when I stepped out of the tent, her black hair pulled into a ponytail that slapped her shoulders as she raced around the crackling fire towards me.

It was some time past sunset, the sky a dark emerald with flashes of red like a hidden fire. It was nice that our camp always looked the same no matter where we were. Even with three new tents, it was familiar enough to push a weight off my chest.

"How do you feel? Dizzy? Sore? In pain?"

"Bothered," I replied dryly, patting her arm. "I'm fine."

"What's all this about a secret?" Jakoda barked from across the fire where she piled grilled meat onto a plate of bread.

I glanced around, checking we weren't missing anyone, and startled anew at Zaugustus's absence. I'd got used to the grumpy old man's beleaguered caretaking over the last two months; it hurt that he was gone, and I'd never see him again.

*You're troupe.*

"Letta?" Ryvan prompted, pushing up off the log he'd been sitting on with Hames, the two of them reading—oh, the bastards had stolen Farrang's journal from me. Rude. "You spaced out."

"I'm fine," I insisted again, giving him a scowl when his

expression filled with scepticism. "I just need to talk to you all. There's something you should know. And if you've read that journal, and it contains what I think it does, you'll understand why."

"Here," Jakoda barked, stalking around the fire and shoving a plate into my hand. "Sit and eat before you waste away. The secret can wait a few minutes longer."

I plopped onto the ground, not caring how uncomfortable it was when I tucked into my meal, and groaned at the taste of salt and meat on my tongue. I devoured it in three minutes flat, and glanced hopefully at the grill on the fire for more. Jakoda let out a long-suffering sigh like she didn't love taking care of us, and put more meat on the grill.

"What's in the journal?" I asked Ryvan. "Anything about a woman compelling human rebels? Or an assassination attempt?"

He raised a dark eyebrow, grabbing the journal from Hames and plopping on the ground beside me. "You wouldn't believe everything that's in this thing. Yes to both, by the way. Apparently there's a power-mad goblin out there compelling the humans that set the theatre on fire, and she's got them locked into some sort of agreement they can't back out of."

"Fun," I said flatly. "How many are there?"

"Rebels? It doesn't say."

"Names?"

"Three, but only first names so they're impossible to find." He sighed, giving me a once-over. "It says her network is so big, she can reach any goblin and human, anywhere."

"So the attack on those soldiers was planned specifically for them," I murmured, stretching my legs out in front of me, the fire warming my calves. "Great."

"Like the Haar wasn't enough to contend with," Hames snarled, his quiet seriousness broken as he glared into the fire. "When I find the bastard who did this, I'll flay them into a hundred pieces."

"*Could* you do that?" I asked with interest, glancing at the big, brawny goblin and his many rings.

He nodded, jaw clenched.

I let out a low whistle. "Nice. And, since I'm getting things off my chest, I should tell you I used my jaguar to track the humans who set the theatre on fire."

"You did *what?*" Jakoda hissed, stomping towards me with her blue hands in fists. "Do you have *any* idea how dangerous that was? You could have *died!*"

"Well, I killed three of them, so all's well that ends well."

"Have a care with your own life, girl," she muttered, heavily disapproving. "You'll send me into an early grave."

I winced, unable to meet any of their eyes. "Anyway, back to the journal. I found that in Farrang's office when I went looking for my necklace. Farrang's the muscly rebel who kidnapped us. Well, he *was*. He's dead now. Valour ripped out his throat."

"Who's Valour?" Cherish asked, her voice hardened.

"My jaguar. The bastards took my ring so I couldn't use magic; I think they were scared of her. But I stole it back and found that journal, plus a bunch of new jewellery and maps of Kier's castle. Wait, where—"

"You dropped them in the basement," Jakoda said, her lips pressed thin and waves of heavy annoyance coming from her. "I got them before we left. They're in my tent."

I let out a breath of relief.

I continued, "I managed to bullshit the rebels so they thought I was on their side and hated all goblins. Blind fuckers couldn't see you guys are my family. Their mistake."

"Aww," Cherish breathed, softening.

Fuck, I hadn't meant to admit that out loud. My face tingled.

A lump swelled in my throat when Jakoda dumped a new plate of meat in front of me.

I ate a piece so I could think through my next words. "You guys hate the Bluescale king, right?"

They nodded fiercely.

"But in all our plays..."

Fuck, this was hard. My stomach twisted into knots around the grilled meat. What if they hated me when they found out I was a royal by marriage?

I took a tight breath and forged on, "You don't seem to hate Kier as much—like in the Haar act, he's the one who swoops in and saves everyone and—"

"Letta," Ryvan interrupted.

Oh, thank fuck. I was rambling, and I didn't know how to stop.

I glanced up—and gulped when I saw I had everyone's attention. Cherish frowned, concern knotting her brow. Hames was as impossible to read as always. Jakoda just watched me with narrowed eyes, her arms crossed. Aerona was the one who worried me; she looked like she'd already figured out where I was going with this confession, her eyes wide.

"So—Kier Kollastus, yay or nay?"

Jakoda shrugged. "He's the best of the lot, but I wouldn't say I like the man."

"The princes are known for cruelty," Cherish

murmured, her eyes distant. "But I haven't heard of Kier torturing anyone."

Except my sister before he killed her. I really didn't want to think about that right now.

Or ever.

"Hames?" I prompted.

"I hate every royal in both kingdoms," he answered in a low growl.

"Equal opportunities; that's fair," I replied, way too upbeat.

"Why?" Aerona asked, her sharp eyes fixed on me.

I dragged a sharp breath into my lungs and said, "This ring on my necklace? It's my wedding ring."

"You're *married?*" Hames demanded. "Where's your sorry excuse for a husband, then? *He* should be the one saving you from bastard rebels."

My mouth twitched into a smile; I ate the rest of the meat on my plate so I couldn't be expected to answer.

"You haven't heard the best bit yet," Ryvan told them with a little smirk, his midnight eyes dancing.

"How do *you* know?" Aerona demanded.

"Remember when we performed in Lazankh and all you lazy fuckers slept in while I went for breakfast?"

"Yes," Hames muttered. "How is that relevant?"

Jakoda watched us both closely, like a wolf waiting for its prey to emerge. "Spit it out, Ryvan."

Ryvan did not spit it out; he gloried in their attention. "I'd just picked up our custard tarts when I got swallowed up in a crowd. Something about an announcement."

"Oh, gods," I groaned.

"While you were all tucked into your beds for an extra hour, *I* saw Prince Kier and his fresh-faced new wife being presented to the people of Lazankh. The princess was in this big, poofy blue dress, like a cloud, *very* hard to miss. She looked prettier on the podium than in real life."

I shoved the flat of my palm into Ryvan's head and pushed him over.

"You?" Cherish breathed, her eyes so wide they dominated her face, making her look even more dollike.

I gave a little wave. "Zabaletta Kollastus, technical princess of Bluescale kingdom. Quick question; do you all hate me now?"

"Hate you?" Jakoda exploded, looking even more pissed off than she had before. "I've half a mind to stab you in the *other* side of your chest for the mere suggestion. You're one of us, girl. You're troupe. We don't hate our own."

Cherish gave me a long look, somewhere between sympathetic and irate. "Don't be crazy, we wouldn't hate you. But are you *really* the princess? The human who signed the treaty and gave us a temporary ceasefire?"

"Ehhh." I wobbled a hand. "It wasn't heroic. I only married him to kill him."

Hames barked a surprised laugh, giving me an appreciative look.

"It didn't work," I told him sadly. "I'm his mate; apparently I can't kill him."

"Mate," Cherish breathed, covering her mouth with a hand.

"I thought mates were made up," Aerona said, frowning at me.

"Nope. Hence, I have to stop this assassination." I looked at all of them, my family. "I need to go back to Lazankh. Will you come with me?"

# 19

"You've lost your damn mind," Jakoda growled, and dropped angrily onto the floor across the fire. It was a power pose, the way she sat, and I envied it. "And you were mad enough before this."

"The city's surrounded by the Haar," Ryvan said gently, squeezing my arm. "We can't get in."

I knew that, but I also knew the Haar wouldn't hurt me.

"We can get in," I assured them, settling a pleading look on Cherish, the soft touch. "I know a way. *Please*. I don't want to go alone."

She groaned, dragging a hand down her face. "If we can find a way in ... *fine*, I'll go with you."

I pumped my fist. "Yess!"

"If you know how to get into the city," Jakoda muttered, still heavy on disapproval, "we'll go as a complete troupe. If the prince can track down these human rebels and take them out, that'll be justice for Zaugustus."

Our conversation drifted to bloodshed and revenge so casually. I loved these people.

Aerona nodded viciously, her brow knotted. "He deserves justice. They should all *burn.*"

Ryvan knocked his shoulder into my good one and grinned. "You know I'm always down for crazy shit. And anyway, you think your prince will give us a boon for warning him about this assassination?"

I was hoping he'd decide not to kill me, but I kept that to myself. "I'll make sure he does. *Within reason,*" I added quickly. "No wild requests."

"Does a mansion on the banks of River Saul count as wild?" he mused.

*"Yes."*

He made a sulky expression, flicking his long brown hair out of his face.

"Hames?" I asked hesitantly. The big man had been silent, and it made me queasy. Everyone else assured me they didn't hate me and this changed nothing, but I knew Hames had lost and suffered and grieved, and he blamed it on the royals of both kingdoms.

But a corner of his mouth flickered up as he met my stare. "I didn't just carry you across five miles and heal your wound to abandon you now."

"Good to know," I replied, choking up, pretending my bottom lip wasn't caving in. "Thanks."

"Awww," Ryvan cooed, stroking my back. "Look, we made the princess cry."

I snarled in his face. "I expressly *forbid* you to tease me with my title. On pain of death."

"Sure, princess," he agreed easily, and grinned as he got to his feet. "Let's pack up the camp, shall we? Get a head start on the trek? I'll get her highness's tent."

I groaned and buried my head in my hands. I was going to regret telling them all the truth.

# 20

"Ruthless gods," I breathed, standing at the top of the forested hill above Lazankh and staring at the city. My home.

I could just make out the solid walls, and the spiked steeples of lapis rooftops, the castle standing taller than every other building. The rest of the city was blanketed in mist, a huge ring of it wrapped around the walls, searching for a vulnerability. The second it—he—found one, he'd swarm the city.

"See?" Ryvan huffed, giving me a look that clearly decreed me mad. "There's no way in."

I set my jaw, staring at the fog, searching for the thinnest place. "There's a way. Stay here."

"While you commit suicide?" Jakoda demanded, grabbing my arm when I set off down the blue hill. She yanked me firmly back up. "You've lost your mind, Letta. We're not letting you sacrifice yourself to the Haar."

"It won't kill me," I promised, touched that she cared so deeply. I held her stare, showing her nothing but calm and confidence. "I've been inside the Haar before. I can't explain it, but just—trust me?"

She worked her jaw, too pissed off to reply.

"The second you sound in distress," Hames warned, "we're coming after you."

I batted my lashes at the big man. "Your confidence in me is heart-warming."

"I'm coming with you," Ryvan informed me, as if it was non-negotiable.

"You're absolutely not," I growled, evading Jakoda's fierce grip on my arm to grab Ryvan. "Trust me, Ryvan. It's not gonna hurt me. *Please.*"

"No," he muttered stubbornly, his midnight eyes full of the same pig-headedness I possessed, too.

"If I go alone, it'll spare me."

"Mother knows how," Cherish said under her breath.

"But if you go, too, the Haar might not let me through." I nearly said *he might not listen to me* which would have brought up more questions than it answered. "Ryvan. Stop being a stubborn bastard."

"I'm being protective of my best friend, you blind prick," he bit out, a muscle feathering in his jaw.

"Awww." I literally melted. "I'm your *best* friend?"

"Fuck off," he growled, tearing away from me and dropping onto his ass on the blue hill and waving a dramatic arm. "Go on then, run off to your painful, tormenting death."

I gave him a double thumbs up. "I will. Back soon! Oh, Hames do me a favour and grab hold of Aerona. I don't trust her to stay put one bit."

Aerona bared her sharp teeth and produced a knife from her coat to point at me. I blew her a kiss, my mood buoyant and excited. At least, until I remembered that

Kier might not want me here, no matter what my dream hallucination said.

When Hames took hold of our youngest player, I gave them all a nod, a quick thanks, and began the anxious walk down the hill to Lazankh.

*Remember the marks on your neck,* I reminded myself the whole time. *Dreams don't leave love bites; it was real. It has to have been real.*

The closer I got to the wall of fog, the more apprehension bit at me. Fine hairs rose along my arms, a shudder zipping down my spine. I could no longer feel the sun on my back; the light wind didn't stir my hair.

"Haar?" I breathed when I got within a few feet of the mist, reaching out my hand and getting deja vu to when I was last in Lazankh.

The second my fingers connected with the fog, the whole wall pulsed, growing thicker, condensing until it was impenetrable.

I'd fucked up.

I hadn't seen the Haar in days. He hadn't come to rescue me from Farrang. What if I couldn't trust him anymore?

"It's Zaba," I breathed, anxiety making my chest tight as the wall of fog shuddered. "Remember me? Zaba?"

*Fuck, please remember me. Please don't kill me when I'm so close to home.*

The fog under my palm moulded to my hand, and I sucked in a sharp breath when it seemed to soften, letting me push through the wall. I tried with my other hand, and the Haar there dissolved under my touch, too.

"Here goes nothing," I murmured, the back of my neck crawling as I waited for something to go wrong.

I turned and pressed my shoulder into the fog,

exhaling a rough breath of relief when it thinned around me and I could glimpse the gates beyond it.

I glanced up the hill to my troupe and made an emphatic beckoning movement with my free arm, holding the Haar away with my body wedged into the gap.

"Come on!" I shouted. "I don't know how long it'll hold."

Aerona and Ryvan were the first to reach the bottom of the hill, Cherish close behind with Hames helping Jakoda keep her balance on the steep slope.

"How are you *doing* that?" Aerona demanded, her eyes wide in her turquoise face and a knife in each hand.

"Who cares? Get in!" I snapped, reaching through awkwardly to push the gate. The iron opened with a low, grating creak that made me jump. My nerves were so damn shredded; I'd never sleep peacefully again. I kept waiting for the fog to resolve into the shape of Kier, but it never did.

Was something weakening him? Stopping the Haar from taking a form?

Aerona pressed as close to me as possible, wriggling her way through the wall of mist and beyond the gates.

"Wait there!" Jakoda barked.

Ryvan gave me a narrow look as he squeezed past me and through the gates; I avoided that suspicious stare and beckoned Cherish through, my heart slamming hard.

"There better be a good explanation for this," Jakoda muttered, giving me a steely look as she brushed past me and into the city, Hames silent and looming behind her.

"Thank you," I whispered to the Haar when they were out of earshot, and then I ducked through the gap in the wall, through the gates, and into Lazankh.

The city where I'd planned to kill a goblin. The city where I fell in love with one.

# 21

"It's a ghost town," I breathed, unable to reconcile the deserted, too-still city with the place I'd ridden into in a carriage four months ago. It wasn't just the bright blue roofs or the painted glass windows that made this city vibrant; it was the voices and laughter, the vendors who'd stopped to stare at Kier's procession, the kids darting through the streets playing tag, the pale-skinned men with sunburned heads, the blue, horned women with excited grins on their faces.

"Would *you* come out of your home if your city was surrounded by murderous magic?" Cherish asked, looking regretfully around the street we walked up, a flask of tea clutched in her hands.

"No," I admitted, flexing my hands at my sides, wanting to wrap my arms around myself. "I still don't like it. Feels like a spirit's going to jump out from behind every building and put a curse on me."

"Curses aren't real," Aerona scoffed, the sound deep in her throat.

I wasn't so sure about that. Being the fated mate of the

man who killed my sister felt like a curse, and I was sure Kier thought the same about me.

*Please don't let him kill me on sight.*

The only good news about the deserted city was there were no guards to execute me for breaking the grounds of my exile.

"Curses are as real as the Mother," Jakoda growled, sounding like she had personal experience with one. "Don't tempt fate by suggesting otherwise."

Ryvan let out a low whistle, cutting off whatever our youngest member had been about to say. "It's still intact."

I followed his stare up the road, and my stomach swooped at the sight of the castle with its tall, grey walls and conical towers, the roofs a pure, royal blue. Gods, the scent of it was already drifting through the air, hyacinths and deep, woody spices. My heart panged.

Cherish ducked closer to me. "Are you okay?"

I nodded silently, tracing the bright silver windows of the castle, searching for signs of life. What if ... what if everyone was already dead? What if Kier was in my dreams because he was gone from everywhere else? What if that was the last remnant of his soul?

"The safe house is this way," Hames said quietly, giving me an assessing glance. "Are you sure you'll be okay? I don't like leaving you."

I mustered a smile. "I'll be fine, don't worry about me. I've already climbed over these walls and snuck inside the castle before; I can do it again."

"Do I even want to know?" Ryvan asked with a laugh.

"I was foraging for poisonous plants to help me kill Kier," I replied, snorting at my troupe's violent surprise. "What? I told you I wanted him dead."

"And now?" Cherish asked gently.

I shook my head, exasperated with myself, with him, with the whole damn situation. "I haven't figured that out yet."

I had, I was just too much of a coward to say it aloud. Jakoda's stare was heavy on me, probably because I'd flippantly told her how I really felt. I didn't think I'd ever confess who my husband was, so it hadn't been an issue.

"If you need help, hang a piece of red fabric from a window on the front side of the castle," Hames told me, watching me with a strange reluctance. "We'll be there instantly."

I nodded, my chest even tighter. I rasped, "Thanks, guys. And sorry for not telling you about ... all this." I waved a hand at the castle.

"Remember," Ryvan said seriously, linking his arm with mine. "I want a house on the River Saul. *Preferably* with five bedrooms, *and* I'd like a room specifically for all my clothes."

"What clothes?" I asked dryly, looking at the bag on his back.

"All the clothes my princess friend is going to buy me," he quipped, fluttering his lashes.

I elbowed him in the ribs. "In your dreams, Ryvan. In your dreams."

I took a step towards the castle, but Aerona darted into my path, a deep scowl on her face. She thrust a dagger at me, and I stiffened automatically, waiting for the attack. It took me a moment to realise she was giving it to me.

"Thanks," I muttered, my throat tight as I took the weapon and tugged one of her braids with my other hand. "I'll treasure it."

"I'm not *giving* you it," she huffed, crossing her arms over her small chest. "It's a loan, and I expect it back."

Was this a bribe to return? My heart hurt even fiercer.

"I'm not leaving you guys," I said, looking at all of them, my strange little family. "I'm coming back, Aerona. Promise."

"If you don't, I'll hunt you down—" she hissed, her eyes fierce.

"And kill me?" I finished, a grin splitting my face. "Yeah, I know. I'm coming back," I repeated, giving them all a final look.

"Be careful," Hames warned, his square jaw clenched.

"If it looks like the prince is going to stab you," Jakoda said sternly, grabbing my arm, "stab him first."

"Will do," I agreed easily. "Any parting words, dear Cherish?"

Cherish was paler than usual; she kept throwing shifty glances at the castle. "Do whatever it takes to survive," she breathed, which was strange advice for someone reuniting with their husband, but I promised I would.

"You better take your own advice," I said fiercely, ignoring my burning throat. "Stay safe; don't go outside the walls. Aerona, no stabbing anyone."

She huffed a breath, scowling at the cobbles under her boots, but she nodded.

"I'll be back soon," I swore, and took a step away from them, my heart aching viciously.

But it wasn't permanent. I just needed to break into the castle without being seen, find Kier without being executed, and tell him there was a murder plot with him at the heart of it. Then I'd be back with my troupe.

Easy peasy.

# 22

The castle was defended by thirty guards, all armed with those modified emerald cannons Xiona had made. The sight of them made my heart squeeze, the thought of what shooting the Haar would do to Kier ramping up my anxiety even more. I knew there wasn't silversweet in them, and I knew the damage it could do. The Haar's scream echoed in my ears.

I crouched in the doorway of a long-abandoned shop, deja vu hitting me again as I watched the guard rotations and waited for a clear break, already planning my route through the castle.

When the guards were safely out of sight, I ducked out of my hiding place, fervently missing my rubber slippers as I made the difficult climb up the tall wall.

"Shit," I grunted when my fingers slipped, and for a moment I hung by my fingertips, the wind tugging at me, taunting me with the threat of falling.

I gritted my teeth and swung my other hand up, digging my fingernails into another hold and heaving myself up, bit by excruciating bit.

At the top, I panted for breath and scanned the grounds, ensuring I wouldn't be spotted. Groaning a mini pep-talk, I swung my leg over the other side and descended as quickly as I could without dropping myself on my ass. I had mortar under my nails, and some of my fingers were bleeding, but I laughed breathily when I dropped down to the grass, a sense of victory swelling my chest.

*I made it.*

Kind of. I still needed to climb up the castle wall and sneak inside, but I knew exactly where to get in.

Nothing had changed since I was last here; the stone was still pockmarked from the Haar's handiwork, some of the towers had collapsed entirely, and there were chunks of mortar occasionally poking up from the grass at the base of the castle. But someone had made an attempt to tidy it up at least, and there was still a clear route up to my balcony.

"Should probably stop calling it yours," I whispered to myself, checking the coast was clear again before jumping and catching myself on a windowsill, beginning the long climb. "At least until you know if Kier wants you dead or alive."

It was fifty-fifty right now, and dreams or not, there was a huge chance he'd try to kill me.

That was why I had the rebels' plans folded up and stashed in my bag; if he tried to hurt me *or* ordered his guards to do the job, I'd produce the map and point out all the rebel's little murder notes. If nothing else, it would buy me enough time to flee to my troupe.

Footsteps crunched the path below, and I froze, my body flattened to the wall twenty feet above their heads. I stopped breathing, my whole body bursting with goosebumps as I waited for them to look up and see me. My magic reacted in a sudden flare, but I silently growled at it to *stay inside my rings!*

I strained to hear the conversation of the people passing below me, but they were too far away to catch anything more than *army* and *mountains.*

I only started breathing again when they were long past me. If Kier didn't kill me, I'd really have to advise our guards to look further than their damn feet.

*Our guards.* Ugh, I was getting ahead of myself.

I sucked in a sharp breath and hauled myself up, hand over hand, until I reached a familiar balcony. I flopped over the railing with a grunt and sprawled on the floor exactly as I had two months ago, when Kier realised I wasn't a sweet wife but a snake he'd let into his home.

When he'd kissed me, and changed everything.

"That bastard," I hissed, giving myself another moment to catch my breath before I dragged myself to my feet. Aches made themselves known but compared to what would've happened if I'd been spotted, I'd come off lightly.

Holding my breath, I pushed the door to my room open. No magical shield crackled; no guards came racing in from the corridor outside, so I inhaled a desperate gasp and closed the door.

My throat burned as I scanned the room, the familiar pale furniture, the white walls and cobalt curtains. Gods, the *smell* of it was still the same. A knot tightened in my chest, gripping painfully. The room was clean, not like it had been stale and unused for weeks.

Had someone else been using my fucking room?

When I found out who, I'd kill them. I might have been unhinged and murderous and a far from ideal wife, but I wasn't replaceable. Kier couldn't just—just bring some other woman in to fill the gap I left.

I was his *wife*.

I strode to the wardrobe and wrenched the doors open, expecting to see someone else's clothes hanging from the rail.

"What the fuck?" I hissed.

My clothes were still in the wardrobe, even my knives hidden where I'd stashed them in the pockets and hem of a dress.

"Right," I breathed, unprepared for the emotion that rattled me. I hadn't been replaced by a perfect goblin bride, then.

Shouldn't he have cleared out my stuff? Kier exiled me, *hated* me. At the very least, he should have slashed holes into the pretty dresses. But it was preserved, exactly as I left it.

"Unlike my bed," I muttered when I closed the wardrobe and turned back to the room. The white sheets on my bed were messy, scrunched like I'd just thrown them off my body and climbed out of it. My pillow was abandoned in the middle of the mattress like an afterthought.

Annoyed at the state of my room, I grabbed the pillow —and something occurred to me, making my chest pull tight. Maybe my bed looked slept in ... because it *was* slept in. Because *Kier* slept here?

"You better be hugging my pillow at night, and not humping it," I growled, resting it against the headboard with its twin, straightening the sheets while I was at it.

Had he really slept here, or was I going mad? I tried to reach along the mate bond in my chest, to feel for the place where Kier and I were bound, but I didn't know what the hell I was doing and all I felt was my own stress. And my *hope,* that damning emotion.

"Only one way to find out the truth," I sighed, and reached into my bag for the folded plans. I held them to my chest like a shield as I reluctantly left my bedroom and strode through the living room into the hallway beyond, making my way through the courtyard that held so many memories.

Too many memories for my fragile heart.

"If you still hate me," I whispered to him, as if he'd hear, "I'm going to kick you in the balls, Kier Kollastus."

I expected the corridors to be silent and deserted like Lazankh's streets, but when I cracked the door open, I sucked in a sharp breath and ducked out of sight. Three goblins in big, poofy dresses walked past, talking in lowered hisses about *the confinement* and *the curfew.*

Well, that explained why everything was deserted outside. Not that it would save anyone from the Haar when the fog finally spread into the city. I needed to speak to that man and give him that ultimatum. Or Kier needed to get his shit in control.

I waited until it was quiet outside and then pulled up the hood of my coat and slipped down the hallways, turning my face away whenever I passed anyone, ducking into empty rooms whenever guards came close.

My heart hammered so hard I felt it in my throat, and I almost backed out three times as I walked down the long corridor towards the throne room. Eavesdropping on several conversations had informed me Kier was holding an emergency meeting.

I could have waited for him to return to his room, could have made a number of different choices, but if I paused now, I knew I'd run away and never come back.

I tightened my fingers around the plans. *Someone is trying to kill him.*

The doors came into view; I sucked in a sharp breath, my whole body electrified. Anxiety carved a home inside my chest, breathing growing more difficult. It didn't help when I spotted the guards on either side of the massive door.

"Meeting in progress," one of them grunted.

On the plus side, they didn't recognise me.

"It's important," I replied, sliding my free hand into my pocket for the rag I'd doused with concentrated sleeproot. "The prince is in danger."

The other, silent guard shook his head.

"Come back later, with an appointment," the chatty one told me, not budging from his position by the door.

*Sorry about this, gents.* I whipped out the cloth faster than they could track. The big guy I targeted first reacted fast enough to stop me, but he expected a weapon or a punch, not a rag pressed over his nose and mouth. He went down instantly, and I sent a strange thank you to the bastards who kidnapped me for teaching me this new concentrated sleeproot.

"You probably won't believe me," I told the second guard as he puffed up bigger, drawing his sword, "but I'm actually protecting the prince by doing this."

I stashed the map under my arm and drew a dagger, ducking around the sudden arc of his sword. I used the flat of my blade to push the sword away from my body long enough to press the rag to the guard's green, tusked face. Fear flashed in his eyes when he sagged and went limp.

"It's just sleeproot," I assured him. "You'll be fine after a little nap."

His sword hit the floor with a clatter the people inside the room would no doubt hear.

He passed out before I could tell if I'd eased his fear.

There was nothing between me and the doors, where Kier waited on the other side. A clear path. A *terrifying* path.

*You can do this,* I psyched myself up. *You can do this. You've done far worse and far scarier things.*

But I wasn't sure that was true. My heart beat so fast I expected it to crack my ribs and fly out of my chest.

I put my dagger away and straightened out the map, keeping the sleeproot-soaked rag in my hand just in case.

*Don't be a coward, Letta.*

Sucking up all my courage, and reminding myself what was at stake, I pushed open the throne room doors. The wood creaked, grinding my nerves to shreds.

I didn't see the people standing along the edges of the room; they were unimportant. My eyes went straight to the throne directly across from me, and my heart legitimately stopped for a second when I saw the imposing figure sitting there. He wasn't blue and furious this time; he was tan-skinned, dressed in heavy black leather, and ... tired. He looked tired.

Heads turned to see why the door had opened on their emergency meeting, and I clenched my hand around the plans, ignoring the way it shook a little, betraying my nerves. I didn't look at the audience; I kept my stare fixed on Kier as I reached up and tugged down my hood.

"I heard this was the place to discuss an emergency." I couldn't breathe when his gaze locked on mine, my whole body shaking.

My voice was breathy instead of fierce when I added, "I'd say an assassination attempt is an emergency, wouldn't you? Human rebels are planning your death, right now. I brought their plans."

I waved the map in my hand, my stomach wound so tightly I was going to be sick.

Kier didn't take his eyes off me. His voice boomed, filling the whole room when he barked, *"Get out."*

Shit.

I swallowed hard, failing to contain a body-wide tremble. He still hated me. Still wanted me dead. I'd gravely miscalculated.

But then he growled, "Everyone! Out *now."*

Everyone? Not Zabaletta? Not me?

Wait ... what?

# 23

*I* numbly stepped out of the doorway as people hurried to obey Kier's command, my heart beating so hard I shook with every slam of it. I couldn't take my eyes off him, couldn't stop the terror and relief choking off my air at the sight of him.

He wasn't dead, he was here, alive. The Haar hadn't killed him; the rebels hadn't got him yet, either.

"Close the door behind you," he barked at the last few people to shuffle out of the room.

The doors closed with a resounding thud that made me jump. And then we were alone, staring across the vast space.

It was the closest we'd been since I learned what Natasya did and he discovered who I really was—and why I'd married him.

Maybe he wanted to kill me in private? That would explain clearing the room. It was the only explanation that made sense. I couldn't let myself hope for more, not now I'd seen him, not now my soul strained to be closer to him.

*Don't get your hopes up, it'll only break you when he rejects you.*

The second we were alone, he exploded out of his throne and strode across the room, his boots slamming the floor so hard each step echoed around the whole room like a war drum, and any hope I'd had that the dreams had been real died a quick, brutal death.

I froze, unable to do anything but stare at him, so full of life and rage and colour. So much sharper than my memories.

"Kier," I tried to speak, but my tongue was dry and the words were like ash in my mouth.

The closer he stalked, the clearer the wrath written in his harsh features became. It drew his brows low over his midnight eyes, flattened his mouth behind his thick facial hair, and clenched his jaw so tightly he was in danger of snapping teeth. It was there in the tightness in his shoulders and the way his hands flexed at his sides. He hated me.

I sucked in a sharp breath when he was close enough for me to see the shine of his dark eyes, the messy strands of his hair and his dark beard that was much thicker than when I left the city.

I finally regained control of my body, but it was too late to take a step back, to run out of the door.

Fierce hands grabbed my shoulder and—and I was hauled into a hug.

"Zaba," he groaned, holding me so fiercely that my soul wept.

What...? He...?

"You came home," he breathed.

A relieved breath punched out of me, and I sank into him with a curse, wrapping my arms so tightly around him that he grunted. His pine and sandalwood scent surrounded my senses, wiping away my anxiety. For the first time in months, I felt *safe.*

"I thought you were going to kill me," I admitted, the sharp edge of pain that had lived in my chest for months easing, leaving only a dull, throbbing ache behind.

"I told you I wouldn't," he replied, ducking his head to trail his nose along my neck, inhaling a long breath of my scent.

"That was a fucking *dream,* Kier," I hissed, resting my head against his chest and not willing to admit it was so I could listen to his heartbeat. "You could have told me the dreams were real."

"I did *try,"* he huffed, his hands flexing against my back, "but you're a very stubborn woman when you want to be."

"Which is constantly?"

"Exactly," he agreed with a soft puff of laughter. "The dreams were real, Zaba. I was there for every moment."

"So ... you don't want me dead?"

He growled, his chest erupting with sudden vibrations that shook my ribs. "I'll kill anyone who even *thinks* about killing you."

My violent heart melted. "It's mutual, Kier. Which is why I'm here. Someone's compelling human rebels and—"

He drew his face from my throat and wrenched me somehow closer, one hand sinking into my hair to grip tight. "I could not care less," he rumbled, and kissed me so hard I gasped.

A groan rose from so deep in my throat that it surprised me, and Kier turned *feral.*

With a dominant hold on my hair, he tilted my head

so he could kiss me deeper, his tongue devouring me. Lip pressed bruises against mine; teeth left claiming marks. I panted, clutching the lapels of his jacket, my head spinning and soul alight with satisfaction and *rightness*.

I let him kiss me dumb for long minutes until we broke for air. Then I sucked down a breath and dragged him back to my mouth, taking full control of the next kiss. The catch in his breathing inflated my ego; so did the desperate way he clutched at me and moaned when I bit his bottom lip, drawing a bead of blood to the surface.

"I missed you so fucking much," he groaned, his hands finding my hips, pressing deep into my skin. "Never leave me again."

"You exiled me," I said against his lips.

"Never again," he repeated in a growl, letting go of me to stoop and—grab the backs of my thighs, lifting me up.

I quickly linked my fingers behind his neck for balance, circling his hips with my legs, and groaned when he walked us across the room, his lips finding my throat.

"I've regretted exiling you every damn day since you left. I owe you so many apologies."

"Damn right you do," I agreed, but with considerably less heat than I intended. His lips on my neck were doing wicked things to me, making my pussy flutter. "You can start by un-exiling me."

"Already done," he replied and sucked a weak spot on my neck.

My hips bucked into his, a breathless sound tripping off my tongue.

"I want—a pardon for my friends. They're little shits. They talk shit about your father a lot."

"Done," he agreed with zero questioning.

Huh. This gave me a serious amount of power.

"I want knives. *And* the sword you owe me."

"You can have my entire armoury," he murmured against my skin, the throne room passing in a blur as he layered claiming marks over claiming marks on my throat.

"But first," he went on, making me jolt in surprise when he lowered me to something cold and wooden, "I'm going to earn your forgiveness."

I frowned to find myself on his throne, not my sad little mini-throne. I didn't realise what he planned until he knelt before me. Before his *throne*. My heart skipped. My pussy throbbed wildly.

But I grinned, sprawling out on his throne and giving Kier a cocky little look as I lifted a boot. "You might need to remove these first if you want to get my trousers off."

Blue eyes flashed, and I knew I'd pay for the show of dominance later, but *fuck* it was so worth it now.

Kier was mine, to order as I pleased.

And I had so many plans for him.

# 24

$\mathcal{K}$ier took his sweet time unlacing my boots and stripping my leather trousers from me, stroking my calves every chance he got. His dark eyes smouldered as he threw the leather aside and grazed my skin with a heated kiss.

"You could've at least folded them," I huffed, trying to hide how turned on I was. My cheeks burned, heat travelling down my chest.

"If they're damaged," he said against my skin, kissing his way up my leg, "I'll personally repair them."

Oh he would, would he?

"I like you like this," I teased, hiding the lust that exploded through me when his nostrils flared. I wasn't wearing underwear, my scent far stronger. "Obedient."

Kier's upper lip curled, a guttural snarl making me shudder. His next kiss landed on my inner thigh with a scrape of teeth, and I let out a moan before I could trap it. His wicked satisfaction was so strong that I felt an echo of it in my chest, and sank my teeth into my bottom lip.

"Obedient for you, and only you," he growled against my thigh. "And only now. Tomorrow, I'm back in charge."

I'd be surprised if he lasted until tomorrow, but I didn't say that. I just threaded my fingers through his long black hair and nudged his teasing mouth closer to my pussy.

"Mother's tits, Zaba," he breathed when he finally noticed my lack of small things. "You walked through my castle like this? People *looked at you* while you were bare under your clothes?"

"Don't growl, caveman," I laughed, secretly delighted by his possessiveness.

"You're *mine*," he snarled. "Only I get to see you, smell you, taste you."

Fuck. Liquid heat poured from me, and Kier's chest rumbled with an animal sound in response. I didn't even need to use my grip on his hair to direct him; he grabbed my thighs, widened them on his throne, and set his mouth upon me with a ferocity that made my hips buck off the cold, dark wood.

"Gods, Kier," I gasped when he buried his face in me, his tongue finding every drop of arousal and drinking it down, tracing sensitive flesh until I tingled all over.

*"Mine,"* he repeated, pressing bruises into my thighs as he ate me like a starving man. Deep noises filled his throat as he licked with fervent strokes.

"Shit," I breathed, tightening my fingers in his hair and nudging him higher, everything tightening inside me when his tongue drew loving circles around my clit.

He was still growling, half feral, and the vibrations shot directly through my nerves until I was trembling.

I couldn't catch a breath, and I honestly didn't care. Heat coiled in my lower belly. I throbbed, ached. Kier's calloused hands travelled from my thighs up my hips and under my jacket, finding bare skin and not satisfied until he found my boobs. When he pinched my nipples, my hips bucked against his face, and he let out a low, thunderous noise that shook my clit.

"Kier," I gasped, everything inside me clenching as his tongue made intent, rolling motions on my swollen bud. "Fuck, that's so good."

I couldn't feel the room's chill anymore; my skin was boiling hot, and shooting higher with every growling sweep Kier's tongue made over my clit. He rolled my sensitive nipples with intent fingers, and the coiling burn in my belly burst into a wildfire.

"Shit—" I choked out, a deep shudder moving through my body, pleasure mounting, threatening and promising all at once.

I tried to gasp his name again, but the sound caught in my throat as my release blasted through me.

There was no describing the relief, pleasure, and satisfaction that tore through my body, intensified by Kier's relentless tongue and his low, animal sounds. I could've sworn I heard relief in those noises, too, could've sworn I felt it in his soul.

He didn't move his mouth from me, guiding me through every shuddering wave until it was over.

I relaxed my grip on his hair, stroking my fingers through it as I came down with a long breath, my eyelids drooping as I gazed at him.

I'd never felt anything as powerful as seeing Kier kneeling before me, clutching me with a frantic desperation as he dedicated himself to making me feel good.

"Kier," I groaned when his tongue made another sweep over my clit, pausing only to lick up everything that dripped from me. I was languid and relaxed, but when his mouth returned to my clit, wrapping around it, I inhaled sharply. *"Kier,"* I warned.

"More," he mumbled, barely dragging his lips from my pussy. "Mine. Mate."

I laughed softly. "Does your vocabulary only consist of *M* words now?"

He flicked a look up at me, danger in those dark blue eyes. He gave one loving lick to my sensitive clit and then sucked me so suddenly that my mouth fell open on a cry and my hips shot off the throne.

"Ruthless gods," I shouted, my legs shuddering, the stimulation relentless. My clit throbbed in his mouth, my stomach rising and falling with fast breaths.

I didn't notice when one of his hands left my nipple until a finger stroked through my wetness and glided inside me. He caressed my inner walls until he found a spot that made me clench around him, and his reaction was so visceral that it speared the mate bond with lust.

"Are you trying to kill me?" I gasped when he sucked my clit with demanding pulses.

He replied with a low sound, electrifying every sense in my body. His insistent mouth dragged me over the edge for a second time, and didn't stop lapping at my pussy until I shuddered and went limp, my breathing deep and even.

I watched through heavy-lidded eyes as he withdrew his finger and licked it clean.

"Happy, now you've ruined me?" I asked breathlessly, my fingers falling from his hair.

Kier laughed abruptly, his voice deep when he said, "Ruined you? I'm far from finished with you, Zaba."

Alarm went through my chest like a shock. My pussy

fluttered, like I wasn't thoroughly satisfied and ready for a nap in Kier's throne.

"Don't even think—"

He didn't let me finish; he scooped me up from the throne and turned so he was sitting on it, me astride him. Without unseating me, he unfastened his trousers and shoved them down his legs.

"Think about what, mate?" he taunted, his eyes smoky with lust. "Making you come again?"

"Yes," I said emphatically.

His wolfish grin sent a trill of nervousness through my belly as he gripped my thigh.

"Just try and stop me," he rumbled, and slammed me down on his cock.

# 25

My jacket ended up on the floor with my trousers. I frantically stripped Kier of his tunic, getting petty revenge by tossing the fine fabric as far across the throne room as I could.

Kier's hands landed on my hips, greedy and squeezing. There was nothing in his eyes but dark desire and affection that bordered on obsession.

I trailed my fingers down his chest, not even circling my hips on his cock. I didn't need to; my pussy throbbed wildly, and by his parted lips and the furrow on his brow, it was torture enough.

"I could do anything to you right now, couldn't I?" I murmured.

"Anything, my princess," he breathed, his pupils dilating as he stared into my eyes.

"Don't look away from me," I ordered him in a breathy tone, and began to move my hips in slow circles.

He sucked in a breath, one hand leaving my hip to squeeze my ass as his cock jolted inside me. With every movement I made, I sank a little lower, his cock hitting a little deeper.

"You're exceptional," he gasped, never breaking eye contact. "Divine."

I bowed over Kier and slammed my mouth into his, a tremor moving through my soul as something clicked into place that had been missing for months. Kier inhaled sharply and grabbed my ass in both hands, grinding himself deeper inside me, setting a faster, rougher pace than I had.

The sinuous motions of his tongue mirrored the glide of his cock until my head spun. I clutched his shoulders, the burning stretch of him fading to slow, gratifying pleasure.

Fuck. I dug my fingernails into his skin, no longer holding back my noises. Giving him everything. Kier rewarded me by lifting me high on his length and dropping me so his cock hit deep, a sudden eruption of sensation making me gouge my fingernails deeper.

"Again," I gasped, not caring that it bordered the edge of discomfort when he filled me that deeply. It was intense, and sated a deep, instinctual need, and I needed *more*.

Kier didn't disappoint, giving me everything I asked for *and more,* until I felt the stirrings of another climax and reached between my legs to speed its arrival.

Kier caught my wrist and dragged my hand away, meeting my outraged stare with something steely.

"You'll take what I give you, Zaba."

"Kier," I whined.

"Keep your hands on me," he ordered, and I wrapped my fingers around his shoulders with a shudder, so hot at the dark tone he commanded me with. "And *I'll* decide if your greedy clit should get attention."

Goosebumps flashed down my spine; I throbbed around him, my pussy clutching him wildly.

"Maybe if you ask nicely," he added, leaning back in his throne and giving me a haughty, commanding stare that made me so hot.

"Please, Kier," I gasped, the sounds of our fucking so suddenly slick and loud.

My eyes rolled back as he drove into me, abusing the angle that made my legs tremble. I needed to touch my clit so badly; I was so viciously close. Just one touch, that was all I needed.

"I said *nicely,*" he replied, disapproving.

A gasp caught in my throat; I pressed my nails harder into his shoulders. "Please, Kier. *Please* touch my clit. I need to come."

"You already came twice," he reminded me, slowing his pace until he was grinding deep inside me, dragging a scream of frustration from me.

"I want to come on your cock," I complained, breathing faster, aching deep inside. "You're being cruel not letting your wife come."

His eyes flashed, a deeper sound in his throat. "My wife."

"Yes," I agreed. "Yours. And your wife would really, really like to come. Please, Kier." Sensing a weakness and aiming right for it, I glanced at him through my lashes. "Please, husband."

"Ride me," he growled, releasing my ass to squeeze my breast. "Hard."

I did as he commanded, my breath catching every time he reached that deep part inside me.

My entire fucking body shook when he found my clit with the soft pad of his thumb. A lightning shock of pleasure crashed through me, and my hips stuttered in their rough motions, my toes curling.

It only took three strokes of Kier's fingers before I collapsed with a cry that echoed off the high ceilings.

"Yes," Kier hissed. "Find your pleasure, my mate."

I moaned, ducking my head as another wave of pleasure gripped me, clenching my inner muscles around him until my eyes rolled back.

"I can feel every shudder of your release," he told me, a little breathless, making steady circles on my clit. "You grip me so well, Zaba."

I wanted to tell him to shut up because every word intensified my pleasure until I thought I would die of it.

"Eyes on me," he ordered. "Let me watch your face as you come."

I groaned, but met his eyes, panting hard and fast in the aftershocks of my orgasm. The dark, possessive gleam in his eyes drew a last shudder from me, and then I collapsed against his chest with a groan.

"Beautiful," he murmured, sliding his hand from between us to wrap both arms around me.

I let out a long breath, all the tension leaving my body until I was calm and ... stable. There was no throbbing pain in my chest, no stabbing ache in the bond. Only peace.

I should probably have noticed that Kier was still hard inside my tender pussy. But I didn't realise what that meant until he kicked off his boots and trousers and stood a few minutes later. Shifting inside me, he drew a gasp from my lips when he began to walk. His hands gripped my ass, keeping me wrapped around him.

"Uhh. Kier?"

I clutched his shoulders, wide-eyed, as he crossed the throne room to the little door at the back.

"I told you I would earn your forgiveness, and I'm *far* from done, Zabaletta."

Holy fucking gods.

## 26

*I* whimpered as Kier strode out of the throne room and down the hall towards our rooms, cold air biting my bare skin. My skin crawled; I was out in the open, where anyone could see my body. There were scars all over me, collected from years of fighting and survival, and I didn't want anyone but Kier to see them.

*"Avert your eyes!"* Kier boomed, holding me tighter as he stormed through the castle. "Anyone who looks at my wife loses their eyes."

The few people in our path spun instantly to face the wall, and a manic little laugh bubbled up my throat.

"You total psycho," I murmured, my skin buzzing less with all the staff turned away from us.

Word must have spread instantly because every person we encountered on the way to our courtyard faced away from us, not a single person risking a peek. Smart. Kier was completely bestial right now. He'd have killed them all.

I trailed my fingers over his shoulders, enjoying the

feel of heated skin and corded muscle. He was mine. He didn't hate me. I got to keep him.

Kier didn't slow his strides until he kicked the door to the courtyard behind him and—my back slammed into cold stone.

I gasped as Kier squeezed my ass, hiking me higher on his waist, and I choked out his name when he drove into me. The thrust was so sudden and deep that I lost control of my body's reactions.

He didn't let me catch my breath, driving so fast and ferociously that all I could do was hold on and moan, sensations ravaging me inside and out.

*"Mine,"* he snarled, so given to instinct that it made the hairs on my arms stand on end.

I dug my heels into his ass, gasping for breath, my eyes wide as his pace never slowed. It was a full assault of pleasure, and I had no hope of fighting the devastating force of my orgasm. A scream crashed up my throat as pleasure wrung my entire body, and I sank my teeth into Kier's shoulder to muffle it.

All that did was make him wilder. Rough hands held me to the wall as he rutted into me, his hip bone grazing my clit and making my eyes cross.

I gasped a senseless noise, a word that might have been his name if I'd remembered how to think.

Kier released a growl that might have been my name. His cock throbbed powerfully inside me, spilling warmth through me in forceful spasms that drew out my own climax.

By the time he stilled inside me and the last wave of my release faded, we were both trembling, holding tight to each other.

"I planned," he panted, "to fuck you hard, and then make love to you for hours in our bed. But I think I'm too wrecked for that."

I laughed softly, my head resting against the shoulder I'd bitten. "Cuddle me for hours instead," I proposed, and wondered just who the hell I was.

"Deal," he agreed.

He slid carefully out of me, grazing my cheek with a lingering kiss before he drew back to stare deep into my eyes. I held eye contact, my breathing slow and steady for the first time in weeks.

"At the risk of inflating your ego," I murmured, skimming his chest with my knuckles, "that was exceptional."

He grinned crookedly, a dimple appearing in his cheek. "I promised to make you scream and melt your mind."

I batted his chest with my hand. "Don't be smug."

"I'm exceptionally smug," he argued, and kissed me, surprisingly chaste and sweet.

When he walked us across the courtyard, past the low couches I'd longed to curl up in for weeks, and up the stairs to our room, an undeniable feeling of happiness bubbled in my chest.

But the reason I was here returned in a rush, and I caught my husband's arm. "Kier, someone's compelling humans to assassinate you."

He drew up short in the doorway to my room, something dark and edged with violence crossing his tanned face.

"And we just left the plans I stole in the throne room. We should probably go back and get them."

His mouth pressed thinner, his nostrils flaring. "If

they're trying to kill me, they'll hurt you if you dared to stand in their way."

"As if I'd step aside while they tried to murder you."

"Stay here," he said, depositing me on the end of my bed. *Our* bed now, I decided. "I'll get the plans. And your clothes," he added, dragging a slow stare down my naked body.

"Kier," I complained.

A corner of his mouth flicked up, incorrigible. "Assassination or not, I *will* make love to you later. For hours. Consider that a promise."

"Someone's trying *to murder you,"* I huffed.

"And my wife is an assassin," he replied, grabbing a pair of cotton pants from the drawer beside my bed. He'd *definitely* been sleeping here. "I'm not worried."

A goblin was *compelling humans* in order to kill him, and he wasn't worried? I sighed with heavy exasperation.

"Kier," I murmured, halting him on the threshold. Maybe because he sensed the shift in my mood. "You need to make peace with your grief. You can't be weakened by the Haar while someone's planning your death."

A muscle feathered when he clenched his jaw, but he nodded. "I'll think about it."

*Think* about it? He needed to *act.* I opened my mouth to argue, but he ducked out of the room. Quick footsteps carried him away.

With a heavy sigh I crossed to the bathroom to clean up.

Until Kier was ready to accept that the Haar was part of him, it was a weakness his enemies could exploit. And they'd already proven they were willing to go to any extreme to kill him.

I groaned, looking at myself in the mirror above the sink.

"He doesn't need humans; he's going to get himself killed."

$\mathcal{I}$ shoved my fingers in my ears when Ryvan let out a loud whistle, my friend staring in wonder at the guest suite Kier had led my troupe into.

"Holy shit, the bed has *curtains*." He spun towards me, a big grin on his face. The first true smile I'd seen since Zaugustus's death. "Letta, look, the bed has *curtains*."

"Impressive, right?" I agreed, laughing when he took a running jump onto the high mattress and Aerona, despite her gloomy personality, did exactly the same thing.

"If there's anything else I can get you," Kier said, hovering at my shoulder with his hand on my lower back, "Just let me know."

"Well, now you mention it..." Ryvan said slyly, flopping onto his back in the plump cushions, "I would *love* a house—"

"No," I cut in.

"—on the banks of the River Saul," he finished, giving Kier a hopeful look.

"Definitely not," I argued, giving Kier a *look* when he began to consider it. "You can have a flat here in Lazankh."

"But *the river,* Letta," Ryvan complained, giving Hames and Cherish a pleading look as they explored the adjoined bathroom. "Back me up, guys."

"Get a bucket and fill it with water," I suggested.

I ducked when Ryvan threw a pillow at my head, smirking when it missed me. Ha! He was still a crap shot. The blood drained from his face when the cushion smacked into Kier instead.

"Your highness, I'm so sorry," Ryvan blurted, fear surrounding him like a physical aura as he scrambled off the bed into a deep bow. "I meant to hit Letta—ah, shit that's assaulting your wife. I mean—"

I grinned, crossing my arms over my chest. "This is hilarious."

Ryvan shot me a betrayed stare.

Kier bent slowly and retrieved the white pillow, so silent that even my fine hairs stood on end.

My troupe froze. Even Jakoda straightened and watched Kier like a hawk, as if she might have to leap to Ryvan's defence.

I raised an eyebrow when Kier inspected the pillow, like the cotton was fascinating. No one was prepared when he threw it hard, nailing Ryvan in the face.

I snorted at the shock on my friend's face. Cherish's mouth hung open; Aerona equally dumbstruck.

"Good aim," I praised Kier, patting his chest.

"Thank you, Zaba." He smiled, squeezing my hip to draw me close again. "Don't worry," he told Ryvan, and glanced at the others, "you're in no danger from me while you're here. You're Zabaletta's friends, which makes you my friends, too."

"Friends of the prince," Cherish whispered to Hames, nudging him with an elbow.

"Much appreciated, prince," Jakoda said in an oozing tone, summoning a smile that didn't hit her eyes. I hadn't seen a real smile from her for days now; I missed them.

"You're safer here than out in the city," I said, my eyes straying to the window and the view of the Haar lurking over the city. My chest tightened; I slid a glance at Kier.

We needed to stop this, and Kier was the only one with the power to stop the Haar's spread. Or at least slow it.

"Thank you for the room," Hames said seriously with a little bow of his head to Kier—and me.

"Don't start bowing at me now," I muttered, but I threw him a smirk so he knew I wasn't really mad. "You've never treated me with deference before, so don't start now."

"You're a princess of the Bluescale kingdom," he grumbled, as if I was the one being difficult.

"I'm still the woman you bicker with, and who put your boots in the pond in Azurann."

"That was *you,*" Hames blurted, his mouth open in surprise. "You let me think it was Aerona!"

"It was her idea," I defended myself.

"You deserved it for making me eat asparagus," Aerona huffed, comically sulky and dark against the pale, fluffy cloud of the bed.

Jakoda smiled, watching us, but she said to Kier, "I'm sure you must be busy, your highness. Don't let us keep you occupied."

Kier squeezed my hip, giving the woman a kind look. Fuck, I'd forgotten how observant he was. How kind he was to his people. "It's no worry. But we'll leave you to settle in."

I shot him a look when he spoke for me, too, but we did need to have a talk about the Haar. I knew he was reluctant, and probably scared, but this wouldn't take care of itself.

I left him standing by the bedroom doorway while I wrangled Aerona into a hug and drew Ryvan close with equal difficulty. Cherish and Hames were easier because Cherish was tactile and Hames froze to the spot when he was hugged. Jakoda gave me a strange, unknowable look I couldn't place until she dragged me close and murmured, "Thank you for taking care of us."

Gratitude—that's what that look was.

"It's nice to not have to look over my shoulder for the Haar every other minute," she added, making me feel like shit.

The Haar was my mate. I doubt she'd be so thankful if she knew.

I cleared my throat. "You took care of me; that shit goes both ways."

"Such a vulgar young woman," she remarked, letting me go and giving me a hard look. "Eat something; you're wasting away lately, Letta."

I groaned, but agreed to get a meal as soon as possible. "I'm fine," I promised her for the third time. "Really. Everything's working out okay."

Strangely, surprisingly okay.

I squeezed her shoulder and motioned for Kier to leave them be, following him through the door.

"Oh, your highness?" Hames called, stopping us on the other side of the threshold. Kier turned back, a questioning look on his face. "If you hurt Letta again, you'll have all of us to answer to."

My eyes nearly boggled out of my head. "You can't just threaten a prince!"

Hames never looked away from Kier, big blue arms crossed over his chest. "I just did."

Kier bristled, but he nodded briskly. "Understood. Thank you for taking care of my wife so well."

He turned his back on my troupe, unaware that I shot Hames a *what the fuck* stare. But my heart was so full and I was so touched and emotional that my eyes were probably soft.

"Needless to say, I'd murder anyone who hurt you guys, too," I said thickly.

"Obviously," Aerona drawled, reclining on the bed and getting out a knife to clean her fingernails.

My heart did a strangle little thrum to have all my family in one place—both Kier and my troupe. We just needed Rook, and everything would be complete. Best not to invite Xiona, or she'd try to murder me.

"No trouble," I warned my troupe, who gave me matching innocent looks, and then I ducked out the door and caught up to Kier. "If they stab someone, it's got nothing to do with me."

He laughed softly. "I see why you're friends with them."

"They're good people."

"They're technically traitors."

I shrugged. "Told you they were treasonous little shits. But if calling out someone for their neglect is being a traitor, that's not such a bad word to me."

His stare slid towards me as we made our way down the quiet hallway, the pale stone reflecting light from a big window nearby. I'd forgotten how airy the castle was, the dark tinge of my memories adding a shadow to these halls that wasn't real.

"You know how I feel about my father," Kier said, glancing at me with a wry gleam. "Maybe I'm a treasonous little shit, too."

I snagged his wrist and drew him to me, leaning against the wall beside the window and stealing a kiss. I'd never get used to kissing him, never get tired of feeling him so close.

*"My* treasonous little shit," I murmured, sinking my fingers into his neat hair until it was suitably rakish.

A throat cleared down the hallway. We broke apart, Kier with a deep sigh and me glaring daggers.

"Your highness," Kier said, drawing straighter at the grave look on his assistant's blue face. I did the same, the bottom dropping out of my stomach. "What is it, Joacaste?"

"It's the human army we've been monitoring through the mountains," she said, not a muscle twitching on her blue face.

I shot Kier a sharp look; he'd forgotten to mention there were humans marching into goblin lands. What *the fuck?*

"They've reached Lazankh," she added.

Kier sucked in a breath and drew even straighter, but I felt his soul collapse with weariness and acceptance. He was so damn strong but so tired, so hurt.

"Thanks for telling us," I told Jocaste in a dismissal as polite as I could make it, resting my hand on Kier's back.

"No more running," I whispered to him when she retreated down the hall. "We need to deal with the Haar. Now."

He let out a sigh of resignation and nodded, a shudder moving through him—unease. And fear.

"I'll be with you the whole time," I swore.

Kier nodded, resigned to his fate.

The only slight issue was the Haar hadn't come when I was hurt in Farrang's office and I didn't have any clue how to call him.

# 28

"I can do this," I hissed under my breath, psyching myself up as Kier and I walked through the backstreets on the edge of Lazankh, the Haar's huge presence hovering over us, pressing against the city walls. Both of us were bundled into thick wool coats, and I had a deep raspberry scarf wound around my neck to keep the worst of the cold from my skin.

The Haar usually responded to me being in danger, but that hadn't worked with Farrang. He'd come when I was sad and grief-stricken, though, and I had no shortage of sadness and grief.

"It might not work," Kier murmured at my side. We didn't have any guards because no one could know he'd created the Haar, however accidentally.

"I could really do without your defeatist attitude," I groaned, giving Kier the side-eye. "Besides, he came when I needed him before."

A low, powerful pulse went through my soul, and my hand flew to my chest to press over the strange sensation.

I only realised Kier had frozen to the spot, rage in his expression, when I walked a step and he stayed behind.

"What do you mean, 'he came to you?'" he asked slowly.

I fought back a shudder and shrugged. "Obviously, a part of you knew I was upset, or in danger, so the Haar—"

"In danger?" Kier exploded, his body vibrating and hands curling into fists.

I bit the inside of my lip, glancing at the rows of terrace houses on either side of us, no lights flickering from their brightly coloured windows. Hiding from the Haar. The Haar who'd comforted me, saved me, and given me a lifeline to hope that Kier would welcome me back.

"I told you the rebels were causing issues in Greenheart," I said, crossing my arms defensively across my chest, the fine wool of my coat jarring. "Their master commanded them to burn down a theatre my troupe were playing at."

Kier watched me with an unnerving intensity and tension. "You got out unscathed."

He said it like that was the only option, or he'd burn down the whole world in a fit of revenge.

I shrugged, the gesture brittle. "I did. But our—we lost someone. Zaugustus. My friend. Probably the only decent father figure I've ever had. He burned to death because of this psycho who's compelling humans, and I want her to pay, Kier. I want her to suffer."

He stormed across the space between us and locked his arms around me, pressing me to his chest so I could feel his warmth and the comfort of a body against mine. "She will suffer for years. I'll make sure of it."

He kissed my forehead and let his lips linger, the point

of contact draining my strength but allowing me to be safely weak.

"I miss him," I confessed, my voice choked. "There's this constant gaping hole where he should be, and he died *for what?* Because some power-hungry maniac wants to turn everyone against Bluescale?"

It hit me then, who was doing this, and I sucked in a sharp breath.

"I've been thinking she was a goblin all this time, but what if the rebels just *think* she's a goblin because she can control them?" I drew my head back, staring at Kier with wide eyes. "Goblins can tell a human from a glamoured goblin by scent, but we can't do that. If we saw a tall, muscular person with magic and no visible object, we'd assume they were a goblin. What if this is a *commander,* trying to win the war by turning Greenheart against you? Sit back and let them attack you, and vice versa, then you wipe each other out!"

Kier ground his teeth. "It makes sense. But that's a problem for later."

"Not with soldiers on the fucking doorstep," I growled, glaring at the high wall that stood between the city and a human army. My breathing raced. "If it's a human, they can be killed."

"Goblins can be killed too, Zaba," he pointed out.

I speared him with a glare, my breathing sharper, shorter. "Thanks for reminding me about your fragile mortality. I *definitely* needed reminding that I could lose you, too."

"Fuck," he breathed, devastated, "I'm sorry, Zaba." He held me tighter. "You're not going to lose me."

"The army of humans beg to differ," I gasped, resting

my head against his chest and trying to breathe. "And—I think I know how to call the Haar."

Kier stiffened, his arms even tighter until I grunted.

"No need. He's here."

I lifted my head from Kier's shoulder, and the last of my air trapped in my lungs when I saw the Haar standing at the end of the street, fog drifting around his ankles as he stared at me with the same devastating expression Kier wore.

When he opened his mouth, I expected him to say my name. Instead, he drew straighter and rasped, "Kier."

# 29

*I* couldn't breathe. My next inhale was jagged and desperate. Panic hit when Kier reminded me he was killable, and it refused to abate. Both Kier and the Haar reached for me at the scraping breath I sucked into my lungs, two sides of the same coin, driven by the same instincts.

The Haar's cold fingers brushed my cheek at the same moment Kier stroked my back, and the world tilted around me. Cold slid down my back, raising goosebumps on my arms. The dark windows on the houses around us were like the gaping mouths of dark beasts. I lost control of my breathing altogether.

"Zaba," Kier said heartbreakingly softly, making me jump by brushing his soul along mine. I still didn't fully understand the bond, but I latched onto it like a lifeline. "You're safe, I've got you. Nothing bad is going to happen."

It would. A commander wanted him dead, and they had enough compulsion magic to control whole groups of humans. Maybe goblins, too. Even though Kier had read the plans I stole from Farrang's office and upped security in the weak spots, I could sense the dark god's eyes on us. Scheming, twisting, setting traps that would snap shut around our throats.

Blue light flashed from under my coat, and for a hazy moment I thought it was Kier's magic. But then Valour leapt from my ring and snarled at both sides of Kier—flesh and mist.

Kier bared sharp teeth and tore me away from my jaguar, pushing me behind himself. I was so breathless that I couldn't explain that she was mine, she was safe.

*Don't,* I rasped to Valour.

Her fierce growl banked to a low rumble. She side-eyed the Haar as she sat by my feet, resting her head against my legs.

"He's ... yours," Kier realised, shock in his voice. Satisfied I wasn't going to be attacked, he resumed stroking my back, murmuring promises of safety until I caught a breath, then another, and a third.

Cold wrapped around my fingers and I startled at the icy sensation—Valour's snarl rising—but it was only the Haar. Oh, he was ... holding my hand. A lump rose in my throat, not helping my whole breathing issue.

But I'd been through a lot these past few weeks; I was allowed a panic attack.

Kier moved a hand from my back to my head, stroking his fingers through my hair until a knot loosened and I could choke out a guttural curse.

"We need to talk," I rasped to the Haar, and tightened my fingers around his. Fuck, he was identical to Kier, his moon-white twin. It was eerie as fuck.

"Talk?" he repeated, glancing between me and Kier, still plastered to my body and radiating worry.

I turned to give Kier a look; he returned it with heavy reluctance but swallowed, a muscle ticking in his jaw.

"You've hurt enough people," he said, looking at the Haar's shoulder. I rubbed my hand up and down *his* back now, sensing how impossibly hard this was for him. *"We've* hurt enough people. Danette's death—" He ground his teeth, his sapphire eyes dulling. "I know I handled it badly, but I never meant for this to happen. We need to— to end this. Undo whatever damage we can."

He jumped when Valour brushed against his ankles, tipping her head back to stare at him. He flicked a glance at me; I nodded, an amused smile curling my lips as he tentatively reached down and brushed a hand over her head and down her back. Her growl cut out, replaced by a deep, engine purr.

"She's called Valour," I told them both. "And I have another baby, a—errr—cat." *Yeah, let's go with cat.* "He doesn't have a name yet."

Valour chuffed through her nose, giving me a judgy look.

"What?" I demanded. "He *doesn't* have a name."

She suggested otherwise, but I was distracted by the Haar's slow, reaching fingers nearing my jaguar.

*Don't bite him,* I warned her.

I tensed when the Haar's hand brushed her back, both Kiers touching her at once. I had visions of hands ripped off, blood spurting everywhere. I tightened my grip around the Haar's fingers, gripping Kier's coat lapel with my other hand.

Valour dropped to the floor and—rolled over, giving them her fluffy blue belly. I groaned at my stupidity.

"We're here to come to find a way to deal with the

human army together," I told them as they knelt, stroking my spoiled baby. "Not indulge Valour's every whim."

She bared her blue teeth at me, and then purred at my mate. I exhaled a sigh and waited for them to be done, ignoring the tingling in my fingers from touching them both. At least I could breathe now.

"I shouldn't have dealt with my grief so badly," Kier murmured, stroking Valour's velvety belly. "I should have faced it. Because I ran from it, you took all my pain and guilt and grief. I can't imagine how badly you're hurting."

The Haar ducked his head, white hair falling into his face as his fingers carded through Valour's fur. "Scared. At first—I didn't know why."

Kier's shoulders slumped, and it hit me how bizarre it was to watch him talk to himself.

"I'm sorry."

The Haar slanted a look at Kier, and I held my breath, the moment stretching out, poignant and significant. "I'm not scared now. They're safe."

Kier frowned. "Who's safe?"

"Everyone." The Haar shook his head and cast a look at the houses around us. "Almost everyone. They'll be safe soon."

*And* that was my cue. I took a step closer, drawing both their attention as I knelt, catching the Haar's gaze. "I know you think you're saving them by swallowing them with your fog, but this isn't the way to do it."

"No one else will suffer," he replied, a sudden growl in his voice. Oh yeah, he was undeniably a part of Kier. He even came with the gratuitous growling.

A smile softened my face, but my chest tightened. "It has to stop, Kier. If you don't stop ... I don't want to see you again. I can't love someone who'd hurt people on this scale. It's *enough.*"

I ignored the hypocrisy of me loving him when he'd *already* hurt so many people. I curled my hands into fists, ignoring the vicious weight on my chest. "Please," I breathed.

"They'll be hurt," he argued, his brows slashed low over his eyes. "If I stop, they'll die like—like—"

"Danette," Kier finished, his tanned jaw clenched. He nodded, giving the Haar an understanding look. "I know you think you're saving them, but there are better ways to keep them safe. No one else will die like Danette did."

No, they fucking wouldn't. I cast a glare at the high stone wall, picturing the army on the other side. It had to be full of rebels, had to be compelled by the commander everyone thought was a goblin. When I got my hands on her, I was going to rip her into pieces.

"No one else," the Haar agreed, fog ebbing and flowing around his knees, brushing Valour but not hurting her. The fog itself had never destroyed anything; the Haar *chose* to. It needed his command to collapse buildings, turn houses to rubble, and massacre whole towns until there was only ashes left.

My stomach turned, memories of Cyana vivid and accusatory. How could I love someone who did that? Ari, the kid I rescued, had escaped that wreckage only to be murdered in the safe place we set up for refugees. *My* idea. My stupid, naïve idea to corral everyone together to make the Haar's job easier.

Kier dragged me from my morbid thoughts by lifting a hand. Valour looked like she wanted to lick his fingers but the Haar moved, startling her into stillness. I froze too when they linked their fingers, deep tan with milky white, both scarred in the same places, flecked with the same hair, both with the same sharp fingernails that hinted at the ferocious goblin just under the surface.

I tried to remember if they'd ever touched before, if the Haar had touched him when he encircled him in fog. My heart thudded against my ribs.

"Kier?" I whispered, talking to both of them.

I took a careful step, my pulse violent in my throat. Valour peeled her lips back from her fangs and crept away from them, brushing against my legs and shooting me a worried look. I absently stroked her head as I made careful steps toward my mate in both his forms.

"Kier?" I reached through my soul to find his, and jerked back at the sharp slice of pain. Agony making my knees buckle. *"Kier!* Stop. Whatever you're doing, *stop.* We'll find another way."

*"No,"* they replied at the same time, with the same voice.

My hands shook as I reached for them, but I jerked back when the Haar's muscular body collapsed into fog.

"No," I whimpered, pressure stabbing behind my eyes.

The pain in Kier's soul throbbed like an open wound, gushing blood I couldn't see. Was the Haar gone? Dead?

No, fog twisted through the air but without a form, without Kier's shape. Pain grew in his soul, forcing a gasp from me.

*"Stop,"* I cried, jerking forward when the fog slammed into Kier's body, absorbed *into* him. "Oh, gods."

Kier convulsed like he'd been shocked by lightning over and over, and I crashed to my knees beside him, grabbing his shoulders when he wavered. He was cold against my skin as his body bucked, tight gasps catching in his throat.

I shivered, terror making me equally frozen. "Kier, stop, *please.*"

Why did I push for this? Why did I want them to talk and reconcile their grief? The rest of the kingdom no longer mattered, and maybe it made me a bad princess but I would have sacrificed every one of them to save my husband.

His lips parted, blue eyes open but glassy, unseeing. "I'm..."

I wrenched him close when he stopped fitting, and held him tight like I could keep him alive by sheer force of will.

"You're not allowed to leave me, Kier Kollastus. Not now or ever."

Valour whined, her purr long dead. I wanted to whine too, but I settled for choking back a panicked cry and digging my fingers into my mate's shoulders. When Kier's irises turned from deep sapphire to milky white, I wanted to throw up.

"Fine," he rasped after a moment. I pressed my lips together to trap a sob when his eyes focused on me. I shook from head to toe, clutching him fiercely. "I'm fine, Zaba. I'm not leaving you, not now or ever."

A sob burst out of me, my bottom lip wobbling. "And the Haar?" I choked out.

Kier paused, his hand resting on my hip. "He's still here. Part of me." Kier let out a ragged breath, his shoulders slumping as he leaned into me. "He's—*I'm* in so much pain. I didn't realise how much I'd blocked out."

I stroked a strand of wavy black hair from his face, shaky fingertips lingering on his skin, unwilling to be parted. "You're okay?"

He nodded, settling his other hand on my thigh—warmer than it had been a moment ago. "I'm okay, mate."

I regained my breathing as I processed that—he was okay, he wasn't going to die—and then thumped him in the shoulder.

"You absolute fucking bastard! How could you do that to me?" My voice was strained and high, still a little breathy. "I thought you were going to die, and I'd be left in this bullshit world all on my own. *Again.* After Natasya and Zaugustus I can't—I can't lose anyone else. So don't you *dare* do anything that stupid again."

I didn't care that this had been sort of my idea. Fear spoke louder than sense.

Kier let me talk, his expression crushed; he gave me an apologetic stare that stamped my heart into dust. "I won't. I promise, Zaba. But you—"

"Yes, yes, I'm the world's biggest hypocrite, and it was my idea for you to talk to the Haar and try to stop the murders. I know. I'm ignoring that because I'm mad at you."

"Because I almost died?"

"Yes!" I exploded, my heart thrumming so fast as I stared at him, caught between wanting to break his nose and kiss him so hard he forgot how to breathe. "You made me love you, and now I'm scared something will happen to you. I've lost too many damn people I love, and I—not you, too. I wouldn't survive it."

Kier grasped my chin, tilting my head until our gazes locked. "You are *not* going to lose me."

My shoulders slumped; my eyes burned.

"I love you so much I can't function without you," he breathed.

"Kier, that's not healthy," I laughed, tilting forward to

claim a kiss. "But I don't work right without you, either. Even when I hated you, I couldn't deny that I loved you. You're in my blood and bones now."

"And you're in mine," he swore, a strange, new softness in his dark sapphire eyes. "Marrying you was the best thing I've ever done."

My mouth flicked up at the edge. "Even though I tried to stab you?"

He shrugged. "That just added a point of interest."

"Idiot," I laughed and kissed him, the world falling away for a blessed minute. "Do you think you can control the fog now?"

His gaze went distant, his hands flexing on my hips. "I can try. But—shit! Zaba, they ... he didn't—"

"What?" I demanded, the cold ground leeching into my legs and making me shudder. "Kier, *what?*"

"He didn't kill them," he gasped, shaking in my arms. "He moved them somewhere safe. He *saved* them." His voice grew small, quiet. "I saved them."

Wait. *What?*

"You're saying the Haar never killed your people?"

"He didn't," Kier whispered, shock leeching through his soul into mine. "He—"

Kier jumped, his eyes shooting to something over my shoulder. The darkness in his eyes were a bad omen if I ever saw one. I spun at the sudden grating of metal, loud enough that I flinched, covering my ears.

Oh gods, the gate—it was crumpling, twisting in on itself.

I flinched into Kier when the gate tore off its hinges and crashed to the ground near the wall with a deafening *boom.* Beyond it, no white fog was visible, only rows of bodies and armour.

The Haar must have been holding the soldiers at bay, and now...

"The army is inside the city." I shot Kier a terrified stare, digging my fingernails into his arm. "They're coming for you."

## 30

For a long, terrifying moment Kier and I were alone as soldiers in black leather armour spilled through the broken maw of the city gates.

"We can't let them get further," Kier said, his jaw clenched and eyes like flint. "Gaia knows *what* they'll do to our people."

The our in that statement made my heart soft, but I hardened myself with a reminder of how many people lived in the city, hiding inside their homes from the Haar, now facing a worse, more ruthless enemy.

The Haar hadn't killed our people; he'd hidden them somewhere they couldn't be harmed. I wanted to press for more information about that, but the railing beside the gate crumpled with a metallic grating and crashed to the ground. *Questions later, defending our city now.*

That word pounded in my heart, my soul—our.

I'd fought through misery, grief, and guilt to get back to Kier. I survived human rebels trying to burn me, Farrang trying to kill me, and one very determined duck trying to peck my eyes out when I unwittingly set my tent over her nest. Against all crazy odds, I was here, *home,* and Kier wasn't just happy to see me, he was damn near ecstatic. I wasn't about to let a human army fuelled by hate, and controlled by a commander on a power trip, take this from me.

"Darling?" I called sweetly to Kier when he unlinked our hands and strode down the street. "Do me a favour and stand there, right where you are."

He shot me a sharp look. "What?"

"You're bait," I informed him, and ducked into the shadow of a tall church with bright rainbow windows and painted steeples. "Now stand there and look helpless."

*"Help, help..."* Kier drawled in his flattest voice.

I stifled a smile, and grabbed the ring hanging around my neck, reaching for Valour and my mouser. *Actually, you know what?* On second thoughts, I unlatched the chain and slid my ring back onto my finger where it should have been all along.

Valour leapt from the band of signet ring, stronger than ever, her outline sharp and clear blue. I silently gestured for her to back up a few steps when her glow spilled around the side of the building. Without being told, she dialled down her gleam and bared her teeth in a many-fanged smile.

"Zaba," Kier warned in a low growl when humans raced at him, swords drawn and pointed outward. No helmets, I noticed. No metal armour. That ought to make things easier.

"Have a little faith, husband," I purred, encouraging my big, furry cat-beast into existence. He leapt from my other ring with a low, rumbling noise; she nudged him with her snout, clearly saying *knock it off.*

He shook his blunt head, his thick sapphire mane ruffling in the wind, and quietened.

*Be ready,* I ordered them. *We're using my helpless husband as bait. When the humans come close, kill them all.*

I swallowed the unpleasantness of killing my own kind to save a goblin. These bastards were my enemies now, and even if it made me a traitor, I knew where my loyalties lay. Kier was my husband, my mate, and my family. I refused to lose any more family.

*Ready,* I warned my fierce companions.

Kier glanced at me, balancing on the edge of nervousness, but he got distracted by the sight of my ferocious mouser. I gave him a double thumbs up and watched his expression flatten even more. His nerves settled though, so that was a win.

*Three,* I counted down, the soldiers close enough that I could hear the creak of their armour and smell the oiled iron of their blades, a scent that threw me back to memories of Natasya cleaning her weapons for war.

Valour nudged my leg, jostling me from the memory and I sucked in a breath. I'd missed *two* in my countdown. Swords were angled to run Kier through, and the whole time he just stood there, a lamb to the slaughter. The trust he had in me was breathtaking.

*NOW,* I ordered my creatures, and sapphire light fired across the cobbles around me as they shot across the road, the aura of illumination around them growing. They seemed bigger, and far more deadly than before. Because coming home had begun to heal my soul?

I shuddered at the sensation of power thrashing like an ocean in my chest, my eyes wide, glossy like I'd just chugged a pint of sugar wine.

Valour and my nameless cat slammed into the front

row of soldiers. I stared, in shock of my own power, as the blue light burned through their bodies until their eyes were empty, blackened shells and corpses dropped to the cobbles. Valour raced on to the next row of soldiers, and then the next, my cat right at her side, hissing at anyone who tried to spear him with their sword.

"*Holy shit,* Zaba," Kier breathed when I came to stand beside him.

"Yeah," I agreed numbly. I'd been training with Cherish, and I knew there was a well of magic inside me, but *this?* Holy shit summed it up.

"Are you armed?" he asked, giving me a hot, lingering stare like he was considering pushing me against the side of a building and kissing me hard. Or burying himself inside me—it was hard to tell which.

I nodded towards Valour and my mouser. "Pretty armed, yeah."

But I didn't have a knife, and I'd never found my dagger after Farrang confiscated it when he kidnapped me. Kier reached behind his back and drew a long dagger from where it laid against his spine, his fingers lovingly brushing mine as he handed it over.

He met my eyes and held for an endless moment, violent shouts and pained screams coming from the soldiers as my magic burned the life from them. We were untouched, but we had moments before they'd be on us.

"We hold the army from the city until backup gets here."

I nodded; he brushed my jaw with his knuckle.

"It won't be long, maybe ten minutes; they'll have heard the gates falling."

"Easy," I replied, only half faking confidence. My magic was wild and unhinged; maybe this really would be easy.

"Don't do anything stupid," Kier warned, lifting his sword into ready position. "I love you with my whole, hateful heart."

I checked we weren't about to be immediately murdered and pressed close for a kiss. "And I love you with all my hateful soul. Be careful, Kier."

"I will," he promised, and kissed me again.

And then he was spinning away from me, diving right for a human who'd miraculously evaded my creatures, crawling along the floor. Kier drove his sword viciously through her back, severing her spine, and then again into the back of her neck until the woman stilled.

My stomach twisted, guilt crawling up my neck. So fast, and another human was murdered. It had hardly taken Kier any effort at all.

*It's them or us,* I hissed at myself. *And I refuse to let us die.*

Even if killing my own kind made me sick.

I couldn't look at the bodies on the floor as I raced after Valour and my mouser, jumping back with a shriek when a broad-shouldered man sliced at my throat. My cat-beast let out a hellish yowl and threw himself on the soldier, clinging with claws sunk into his leg and blasting him with enough blue magic that his eye sockets smoked.

"Thank you, baby," I said a little breathlessly.

He purred loudly, his tail forming a cute little question mark as he trotted away to his next victim. Wait, did he—did he think his name was Baby? He was three times the size of a normal cat, had a lion's ruff, plus vicious teeth and claws that could gut a goblin.

But why *not* call him Baby? If he liked the name, it was his.

I sucked in a breath when a shadow moved behind

me, and I spun on instinct, bringing my new dagger up—
and halting it with a strangled gasp.

"Are you *mad*? I could have killed you!"

Rook stood there with a grin on his brown face and his
eyes creased until they almost disappeared. He was
exactly as I remembered, his dark locs pulled into a knot
at the base of his neck, his tall body draped in heavy blue
leather and decorated with so many weapons and potion
bottles he was like a walking armoury.

"You're back," he exclaimed, smashing a potion bottle
in the direction of a blonde human who'd crept up at my
left. Fuck, I needed better spatial awareness.

"I'm back," I agreed, and drove my blade into an
armoured man before he could cut me. I dragged the
knife through his neck and let out a cry of surprise when
my rings flared cerulean blue and the blade glided
through sinew and bone, cleaving his head off.

I gave Rook a wide-eyed look, swallowing hard. "Any
tips on using magic would be great."

"Trust yourself," he replied, and jabbed a knife at a
soldier who tried to get past us, already reaching for
another potion.

"Oh, great advice. Thanks," I drawled, sucking in a
breath when Valour's glow expanded, throbbing like an
explosion waiting to happen.

A sharp whistle had my head whipping towards the
road behind us, and a physical weight fell off my shoulders at the sight of my troupe. Every one of Hames' rings
glowed, a tidal wave of dark, dark blue forming around
him, and Cherish's bright turquoise pulsed at his side,
ready to take flight. Aerona and Jakoda had weapons in
each hand and matching vicious expressions, like two

generations of the same fearsome woman. In the middle of them all, Ryvan practically skipped, brutal excitement on his sharp face.

"Someone call for the cavalry?" he shouted, inappropriately giddy.

"Hold the line!" Kier yelled from deeper in the army, him and Valour cutting a line through the ranks of human soldiers. "Help me push them back out the gates."

I nodded, the command sending a tremor of nerves through my belly. That clipped order made it real and clear that this was *a war* more than anything had since the gates buckled. We could die here. It wasn't just my irrational—or *rational*—fear of losing Kier, but the reality of battle.

Someone would die, and I wasn't prepared for that.

Hames's dark blue magic joined the beacon of mine, his a force of nature to my vicious beasts. I jumped when Cherish's hawks soared above us with powerful wingbeats and high, visceral shrieks.

I was so distracted by the shadows their wings cast over us that I missed the nimble figure slipping up behind me until steel pressed to my throat.

I froze, my breathing cutting out, my instincts *screaming.*

"Hello, traitor," a low voice purred. My breathing kicked back in with a rush.

"Xiona," I groaned, pushing the knife away from my throat now I knew it wasn't intended to kill me. She'd only hurt Kier by doing that, and as Kier's best friend, no way would she do that to him. "Delightful to meet you again."

If looks could kill, she'd murder me where I stood. I shot her a quick glance, deflecting the short blade of a soldier when it jabbed at me. She looked *exactly* the same as when I last saw her two months ago—short, striking, and pissed off. Her honey-blonde hair slashed short near her chin, her rosebud lips were pressed into a thin line, and hate sparkled like sunlight in her amber eyes. Good to know we were still on friendly terms.

"You're lucky I didn't kill you on sight," she seethed, and without looking threw a lightweight knife into the eyeball of a female soldier who made a beeline for us.

"Yeah, well," I replied, inhaling sharply when someone drove their sword into Baby. He let out an almighty yowl, but it was a sound of rage, not pain, so I resumed breathing. "You can kill me later."

"You hurt my friend," Xiona growled, her eyes flashing as she flung another knife, nailing someone in the throat. They were incinerated on the spot, crashing to the ground as lumps of charcoal. Nice; I wanted one of those.

"He hurt me first," I firedback, gasping when Cherish's hawk dove suddenly and exhaled a plume of blue fire on the soldiers beyond the gate.

I flung my soul across the street, searching for Kier and only breathing again when he sent a reassuring brush back. I scanned the chaos of magic and swords for my friends, panic relaxing its tight grip when I spotted Jakoda, Cherish, Hames, Aerona, Ryvan, and Rook. Xiona was still beside me, debating stabbing me in the throat. We were all okay.

But for how long?

As if the gods had heard me, a spark of green magic hit the air beyond the gates, making even Xiona freeze for a moment. The spark became a flicker and then a full, raging fire, and my chest tightened like there was a lead weight sat on it.

"The humans have brought magic," Xiona breathed.

I shook my head, letting rage devour my fear. "No. The person compelling them is here."

And she wouldn't stop until Kier was dead and Bluescale was hers.

# 31

I was sick and tired of power grabbing assholes. Power was why this whole war started in the first place; humans staked their claim on land that belonged to goblins, goblins pushed back and claimed human land, and now it was a giant pissing contest that killed millions every year.

Feuds like these only brought misery. I should know; I'd married Kier to kill him *because* of this feud. Killing the commander who'd compelled this army wouldn't end the war—it would feed into the vicious feedback loop of violence—but it would save Lazankh. It would save Kier. I wouldn't be terrified a maniac would spring out of the shadows to kill him because he was the last living Kollastus.

At least, the only one who wasn't hiding like a coward.

"Out of the way," Hames' deep voice called to Kier and Rook, who fought to push back the front line of soldiers.

"Who the fuck is that?" Xiona muttered, baring sharp teeth in the face of a small, human woman. She took one look at Xiona and bolted; I couldn't blame her.

"My fucking friend," I shot back, and plowed through a tangle of soldiers, cutting my way through.

I bit back a cry when pain tore through my side and down my hip. Hot blood soaked through my coat, wool doing little to defend against steel. At least my leather trousers stopped the knife harming my leg, but it was little comfort when pain raged like a brand.

Deeper in the army, Kier roared a loud, guttural noise that made me want to flee Lazankh, the goblin lands, and the whole continent.

I hissed through my teeth, fury and agony merging into one hot emotion. When the bastard came back for a killing blow, I moved faster, hacking my knife through his dark throat. Blood splashed my face, hot and viscous. The coppery taste filled all my senses until I choked on it.

The wound blazed like a fire, razing my nerves, but I couldn't stop fighting. If I stopped, I was dead. When another soldier came at me with a spear aimed at my stomach, I kicked his knee, knocking him back until he met Xiona's sharp knife and even sharper smile.

"Hey!" Ryvan shouted, and my head snapped up when he added, *"Princess.* Don't forget who your best friend is."

He was threatened by Xiona fighting at my side? Gods, he was insane.

I gave him the middle finger, my ring glowing brighter as I knocked a blonde man's sword aside and slammed a fist into his stomach. Leather resisted the blow, snapping bruises across my knuckles, and he moved faster than I predicted.

"Shit," I snarled when he drove the point of his sword at my bleeding side. I evaded, but not fast enough to avoid it altogether, and pain made my vision waver. The slow trickle of blood became a pouring rush. "Fucker."

"Traitor," he spat right back at me.

*Valour!* I ordered, gritting my teeth against the building pain and ducking low. I screamed through gritted teeth, ignoring the bright white that burst across my vision to jam my dagger into the bastard's gut.

But he didn't back off, and he didn't drop to the cobblestones when I opened a messy, ragged wound.

I rose unsteadily and backed up a step, *hating* to retreat. Blue light stormed towards us, big enough to cast a glow over the whole street. I caught my breath, but it wasn't Valour; she was still blasting her way down the road, sliding soldiers apart with her claws and jumping over their bodies as she fought to reach me. Too slow to save me.

The rich, sapphire magic that blotted out the sun was a *dragon*. It was ten times the size of Cherish's nightmare hawks, and deafeningly loud as it parted huge, fanged jaws and screeched in pure, murderous rage.

I stumbled away, primal fear making my bones rattle despite the magic being blue, obviously an ally. I was a human, and humans tended to run to the hills when they saw a twenty foot dragon made of violent blue power diving at them with jaws open wide.

A squeak caught in my throat at the close-up clarity of its teeth, every scale on its body shining and pearlescent, its eyes a rich, deep blue flecked with silver and full of strange intelligence.

Valour skidded through a group of humans and growled at a woman who edged a little too close to me, snapping her jaws and taking off the woman's fingertips. I watched from the corner of my eye, too consumed with the sight of the sapphire dragon's open maw as it dove from the sky and—and swallowed the blonde bastard who'd called me a traitor.

"The Mother," someone breathed behind me.

"The goddess came to save us."

"Gaia is here."

*"The princess.* She saved the princess."

With Valour keeping the soldiers away with her viciousness, I slammed a hand over the gushing wound on my side, putting pressure on my bloody skin. The dragon swallowed the blond soldier whole and I could only stare.

Where the hell did Xiona go? I could've used her as dragon food.

*"Nice* dragon," I soothed, giving Valour a silent order to back up and repeating it to Baby when he raced to my other side and—nope, he ran *past* me and cuddled up to the dragon's immense leg.

"What the *fuck,* Baby?"

He rubbed his face on her scales, purring at the top of his lungs.

I threw my hands up in exasperation. Fuck, I shouldn't have done that; I grunted at the stab of pain through my side, my knees buckling for a second. Valour shot me a concerned look, but I waved her off and panted through the deep fire of pain as she tore into another human soldier.

"I've got you," a welcome female voice breathed, and an arm banded across my back as Cherish took some of my weight off my pained side.

"Hello, beautiful," I rasped, giving her a passing attempt at a smile. "Perfect timing."

"The mother saved you," she breathed, staring in reverence as the dragon unleashed a torrent of blue flames upon the humans blocking the gate. Even metal and stone melted under that fire.

Unease stirred in my gut, but it evaporated a moment later when Kier strode past the dragon. He didn't slow his rapid strides, didn't look away from me until he was right in front of me.

"Thank you for protecting my wife," he told Cherish with a dip of his head.

She caught her breath, her blue face darkening around the cheeks. "O-of course, your highness."

I snorted, but I was aware of the ground tilting, and blood loss getting to me.

"Hames!" she yelled so loud I groaned.

She turned to search for him as Kier gathered me close, brushing sweaty hair out of my face.

"Hang on, Zaba," he murmured.

I rolled my eyes, letting my head fall on his shoulder, filling my lungs with his comforting scent.

"This? This is nothing. I've been stabbed *way* worse than this."

Kier and the dragon snarled at the same time, the ground shaking with the force of their fury.

"I want you to go back to the castle," he rumbled, staring into my eyes, not glancing at the soldiers swarming around us for even a second. Whoever got close was ripped apart by Valour, Baby, or—or the dragon. She was Kier's beast, like they were mine. No wonder she'd eaten a guy to protect me.

"Everyone needs far fetched dreams," I replied to Kier, patting his chest. "Not happening, prince."

He began to argue, but a sudden *boom* startled him into a growl. He twisted us away, wrapping his blood-soaked coat around me and cradling the back of my head.

I jumped, sweat beading on my forehead and upper lip as the hollow *boom* sounded again, and again.

"The drums of war," Kier said gravely. "They came here to kill us all."

But why? I could understand the human army claiming the outer towns and cities that had been emptied by the Haar, but why be so damned determined to move *this* far inland? It was a personal vendetta as much as a power grab.

*Valour,* I ordered silently, and my jaguar roared and leapt back into the fray, mowing her way through humans, ripping off limbs, tearing through throats.

"We need to go out there and find whoever is controlling them," I told Kier. "The humans might give up and go home if the compulsion is gone."

"Might," he echoed, his jaw clenched.

"Do you have any better ideas?" I demanded.

"You go home, get in bed, and heal?"

"Other than that."

"No," he sighed, and pressed his lips to my temple, uncaring that we were in the middle of a brutal, bloody fight. We had friends and familiars around us. It was selfish to take this moment, but I'd never been selfless so I took full advantage of it.

"Do not," I growled, grabbing the back of his head, "die, Kier Kollastus."

I kissed him hard and fast.

"On my honour as your husband, I promise to live," he vowed, making my heart skip. He glanced over my shoulder, eyes hard. "You two, stay with her. Protect her."

"Yes, sir," Cherish replied instantly, hurrying closer to me as the crowd surged, carrying all of us out of the melted gates and into the long sloping field full of blue flowers.

Goblins clashed with humans, and I *knew* the violence around us—blood and blades were as familiar to me as my own heartbeat. But this frenzy and scale was its own feral, cunning monster, and it pressed in on me on all sides.

My blood quickened, a chill going down my spine when I saw the full size of the army waiting for us.

I'd naively thought we'd already handled half the army. We'd barely made a *dent* in their numbers, and out here green sparks split the air as soldiers used magical objects to counter goblin power.

And somewhere, hiding, the puppet master watched it all.

I tried to search for her as we flowed onto the field, but a spear raced at my throat, and all I could do was parry the blow and fight.

I could no longer tell if this was a battle for Lazankh or a fight for survival.

# 32

*R*yvan was a comforting presence at my back as an eruption of magic crackled through the air to join mine—a strange bright teal, more green than Aerona's turquoise. He caught me looking and glanced away, his throat bobbing. Guilt crossed his face.

"You're *Greenheart?*" Rook demanded, spinning to pin Ryvan with a hostile glare that made my heart jump in surprise.

I pointed my knife at the pretty bastard. "Watch your tone."

"I'm both," Ryvan spat defensively. "And trust me, I hate it as much as you do, but I need my magic right now. So are you gonna throw a tantrum, or let me defend your damned city?"

Rook's mouth snapped shut. He nodded with zero complaint.

*You go, Ryvan, you go.*

I was in no position to judge someone based on family or birthright. My uncle was a mean, callous bastard, my sister killed an innocent girl, and Lucrecians had been slaughtering goblins for as long as I could remember, mostly for greed. I had no moral high ground.

"Pretty," I remarked when Ryvan slashed his hand and sent an arc of severing magic through a group of humans, like a super-sized, glowing scythe.

"I just killed seven people," he bit out, "and you think my power is pretty?"

"Not as pretty as your face, obviously," I said, earning a growl. But the uncertainty left his face, and he snarled at anyone who did a double take on sight of his magic. Now I knew what I was seeing, it was easy to spot the emerald glow through his azure magic, both sides of his heritage on display.

He grinned as his power took out another swath of rebels, but the smile died when emerald magic blasted from the back of the human army, far too powerful to be from a ring or pendant. Unless you were a human like me. Unless you were the mate of a goblin.

My heart pounded faster as the power crested like a wave, rising over where Bluescale goblins with compelled humans, more of our guards pouring through the gaping city gates to help. Citizens took up arms and magic, and joined us with defiant snarls on their faces.

"Shit," Ryvan breathed.

I threw a panicked look around, not sure where Cherish had ended up, and unable to find Kier, too. But when the green wave dropped from the sky, swallowing humans and goblins alike in bright, violent power, I aban-doned my search and *ran*.

It wasn't thought or logic that drove my body; it was pure, terrified instinct.

Ryvan and I got separated, and I lost Rook, too as I raced to avoid the wave's path, the high wall at my right and blistering green magic on my left. Air burned in my lungs, short with panic. Wherever that wave touched down, people *screamed*. The piercing human screams were the worst of all, but goblin screams were louder and carried further, haunting and shrill.

I pressed my hand to the screaming wound on my side as I ran, and plunged into my bond with Kier, sending a frantic plea. *Tell me you're alright, tell me you're alright.*

The tether shuddered with a response, but it was faint compared to the stern tug earlier. Why did he feel so weak? Oh god, had the wave hit him? Was he *inside* it?

I pushed my body to its limit, pain shattering through my side and up my ribs, another flash of it stabbing my ankle when my next step landed wrong. My leg buckled, and I lunged into the wall to my right, grabbing on for dear life. I kept upright, but my hip slammed into the solid stone, and my vision flashed white. I screamed, agony erasing everything else in the world.

When my scream died, the howls of dying soldiers and our own guards made me flinch. It was so much worse when I couldn't see.

I panted through gritted teeth, riding out the excruciating torture until my vision flickered back, the world horrifying and emerald, the wave of magic so close it could swallow me.

I gritted my teeth and shoved off the wall, throwing myself into a run. Hot and weak, I pulled rough panting breaths through my nose, sprinting faster. The world blurred as pain reigned my body, but I couldn't stop running. The air crackled around me as the lethal wave neared, so devastatingly close.

It brushed my skin, and power sank into me, razing my whole body like emerald fire. I froze between one step and the next, my mouth open but my scream unformed.

Brutal, stabbing magic swallowed me from head to toe, and my eyes bulged at the vicious, blistering pain, tears burning tracks down my face. A choked breath was the only sound I could make. I'd thought a stab wound was painful, but *this* was true and total agony.

A scream rose in my chest, pressure gathering on my lungs like a storm, but it never formed. I choked out another strangled groan, so terrified my blood ran cold and I knew this was it, the end.

The tether between me and Kier went silent and strangely still, not even the muffled echoes of his rage reaching me. I couldn't feel Valour and Baby, either, and fear silenced even my choked sounds. Was I already dead?

A roar of fury reached me, but it was strangely hollow and distant, like I heard it through an echo chamber.

I waited for the pain to float away, for the ruthless gods to carry me into the afterlife, but if anything the pain *spiked*, and—

I realised my scalp stabbed with the bone-chilling sensation of being dragged by my hair.

The pain in my body was one thing, but not being able to see or hear who dragged me was *terrifying*.

I had to still be alive, though. Didn't I?

I tried to struggle, but my limbs were numb and dead. Was this even happening? Was I still in the emerald wave?

I tried to snap a fist at whoever was dragging me, but it was a useless attempt. My body resisted me, refusing to move. I strained against the magic keeping me immobile —because it *was* magic, not simply paralysis from pain— and imagined sapphire daggers I could sink into the bastard who dragged me.

I seethed, gathering rage like armour, bristling inside my own skin. I heaved on my hand again—and gasped when my arm moved *and* I actually made the sound.

I tore myself off the grassy ground and spun, throwing my glowing hand out at—

Rats.

A hundred glowing verdant rats. Oh shit.

I'd been kidnapped by the woman who wanted my husband dead.

## 33

*I*t took me a millisecond to realise with my renewed movement, I also had control of my magic. I didn't have time to call for Valour and Baby; I gave a hard, blunt yank on my magic and when the rings on my hands flashed to life, I punched blue magic into the swarm of rats. *Sorry, babies, it's not you I want to hurt—it's your master.*

Five of them scattered, screaming, but the rest came at me with renewed determination and anger.

But they paused, as one, when a sweet female voice called, "Stop."

The sudden halting of motion sent cold down my spine, and I paused with my boot raised, poised to crush a rat out of existence. *She's here.*

I spun, a growl in the back of my throat—and frowned at the petite, sweet-faced woman who strolled towards me. She had fire-red hair, skin as bright green as the forests between Bluescale and Greenheart, and a face that would set even the gruffest warrior at ease.

"You...?" I asked, a furrow carving between my brows.

No way was this small, fragile woman controlling this many people.

"Me," she agreed in a voice like a goddess.

A strange awareness uncurled through me as we stared at each other, her sizing me up and me staring at her beautiful, delicate features—before my eyes snagged on the green diamond crown on her head and my stomach sank so fast I stumbled back.

"I can't help but notice your choice of accessory," I breathed, a tremble moving through my hands.

A crown—of *emeralds,* the stone of Greenheart kingdom. This was their queen. *The Greenheart queen* wanted my mate dead, a woman so powerful she ruled a whole damn kingdom. I couldn't breathe. We didn't stand a chance.

"You don't have a tiara, I see," she replied, her voice so disarming that I had to remind myself she was a threat—and a terrifying one. She'd made this wave of magic; she was responsible for the screams I could hear beyond it. Somehow, the rats had dragged me to the other side of the vicious crest, and I couldn't see a single person through its bright glow. "How sad."

Her barb hit as intended, and I had no shame in giving the Greenheart queen the middle finger. "It's in transit."

"Deliveries are *so* slow these days," she replied, fiddling with the pearl-encrusted sleeve of her pretty dress.

"Cute," I remarked, yanking hard on my magic and calling Valour and Baby to me. "Your harmless, little routine."

I didn't let my unease show when she smiled and batted her long lashes. Her eyes were a vivid, piercing green that made my stomach flip, and the nausea was exacerbated when Valour didn't rush to my plea. I felt nothing—absolutely nothing—from my mouser.

I was ... cut off.

"Coming from an expert in harmless routines," the queen purred as she glided closer, the train of her dress dragging across the blue grass, "the compliment means a lot."

*I'm going to stab you over, and over, and over. What I'll do to you will make the deaths happening behind me look like a paper cut. I'll rip your intestines out through your belly button and—*

"Bold of you to threaten a queen," she remarked, taking another smooth step closer. I wanted to back up, but I wouldn't give her the satisfaction.

I couldn't avoid my sharp intake of breath, though. "I didn't threaten you."

I didn't. All my threats were internal. Cold spread through me, making my hands tremble. *Valour,* I screamed. *Baby! Come the fuck on!*

The queen smiled, her cheeks round and sweet like she was a doll. "I'm in your head, princess."

I jerked back, clenching my hands into fists and dragging power from my rings. They erupted with a blue glow; relief left me in a jagged breath.

The queen—Cleodora, the notoriously violent woman who scared the roughest of goblins—watched, smiling and unworried, as I shaped a crude dagger and flicked my wrist, hurling it end over end. It sank into her chest, all the way to the hilt.

She glanced down at the knife, and I froze. Air crystallised in my lungs. She wrapped her fingers around my magic and smiled deeper, dimples appearing. It should have been impossible—it was *my* magic. She should have been screaming, not drawing the dagger out of her chest with that sweet smile not flickering an inch.

"You're everything I expected you to be," she told me, and crushed my knife in her fingers. Blue dust drifted to the ground.

I staggered back, clutching my chest as a new, sharper pain cut through me. It felt like a scalpel sliced me in fast, precise lines, like she'd cut out a piece of my magic. A piece of my soul.

"Impulsive, hot-headed, violent," she went on. "No one mentioned you were so loyal and protective, though. How surprising that you returned to warn your husband when you hate him so much."

"Yeah, well," I spat, backing up a step, my pride crushed along with my magic, "the line between love and hate is as thin as a blade. Question—what the fuck do you want?"

Why wasn't I dead already? She was toying with me.

"In the grand scheme of things," she mused, backing me up against her wave of crackling emerald power, "I want what I'm owed: the entire goblin lands. I'm ambitious, I won't deny that. Queen of Greenheart is impressive, but Queen of the Goblin Lands? It has a much better sound to it, don't you think?"

She was close enough for her breath to fan the fine hairs near my scalp. Good. I reared my head back and drove my forehead into her face, breaking her nose with a satisfying crunch. Pain blast through my skull, but this wasn't my first headbutt, and I recovered faster than Cleodora.

"What I *think* is you're a power-hungry maniac," I spat, slamming my fist into her stomach to wind her and gritting my teeth as pain and dizziness flared at the movement. Gods forbid my wound let me have a single moment of strength without sapping it from me. "And I'm not letting you touch a single fucking hair on my husband's head."

"Sweet," she said, seemingly genuine as her doll-like face softened. She didn't have tusks or horns, only claws that could pass as fingernails. Her beauty only made her stand out more; it made her deadly. "But entirely futile. I'm in your head, Zabaletta; you couldn't hurt me if you tried."

"I just stabbed you with a magic knife," I pointed out, wrenching on my bond with Kier, screaming commands at my magical creatures. There was nothing—only echoing silence on the other end.

"A harmless knife," she replied with a laugh. "Hold her still, gentlemen."

"What?" I threw out a fist, spinning, searching for the next assailant. But I focused too high; the attack came at my ankles, and too fast for me to escape.

Rats made of deep, emerald green piled on top of one another, trapping me in a mountain of magic and fur, teeth sinking into my legs, so much more solid than any magic ought to be.

I slammed my fist down, but for every rat I punched aside, three more replaced them until I was surrounded up to my thighs. Trapped with barely an inch to move. Panic clawed up my throat, claustrophobia hitting so fast that my head swum.

*Kier!* I yelled, hauling on the mate bond.

"It's sad that you think you're really doing that," Cleodora remarked. "You do nothing without my permission, Zaba."

"Don't call me that," I growled, my breathing fast and

short.

"Because only *he* calls you that name?" she asked, shaking her head. "He and the abomination he created."

"That's what all this is about?" I demanded, trying to kick my legs free and failing so spectacularly that my whole body shook with fear. "You're scared of the Haar?"

"Oh, no," Cleodora replied with a smile. "Actually, I admire the destruction. I'd love to know how he did it, so I can make something similar. Rather than fog, I feel an affinity for fire. Imagine the whole goblin lands razed to nothing, then the greatest empire the world has known built from the ashes."

Oh good, she was a hundred percent insane. "You'd hurt your own people?"

But she already had—she killed her soldiers in the coliseum so she could pin it on Kier and push the hunger for a goblin civil war.

Cleodora shrugged. "I'd rather not, but it's an inevitable result of growth. Anyway, that's enough chit-chat. Look me in the eye, Zaba."

I slammed my eyes shut, contrary to the bitter end.

*Kier!* I screamed. *Valour! Baby! Fucking anyone!*

If the ruthless gods were watching, their backs were turned to me. They didn't intervene.

My eyes opened against their will, and the queen smiled as I slammed them shut again—only for them to open. It wasn't a fight, wasn't a battle of wills. It didn't even feel like a parasite in my body; everything felt completely normal except my eyes opened without my consent. This time they stayed open, and Cleodora caught me in a stare.

"Good. Now listen carefully, princess. You're my eyes and ears inside the castle, or wherever else your husband and his entourage go. If you give *any* indication of being under my control, I'll slit his throat from edge to edge and give the same treatment to your actor friends."

I hissed out a breath, my teeth bared and cold panic drenching me from head to toe. I opened my mouth to hurl a violent, graphic threat at her, but my lips pressed firmly shut and refused to move when I told them to.

"If you fight the compulsion," she went on, "your mind will tear itself apart. It will be excruciating, so I'd advise against it. When I contact you, you'll find somewhere private and tell me everything I want to know."

She patted my cheek. I flinched back. It was the only bit of control she allowed me over my body.

"If Kier gets even an *inkling* that something is wrong, I will hunt down everyone you love. Nod if you understand."

I bared my teeth, magic sparking in my rings, but I nodded. She had me by the balls, and I didn't know how to get her out of my head.

"Now," she said brightly. "In the unlikely event that someone discovers my compulsion, you'll kill yourself before you speak my name."

I glared at her pretty face, bile splashing up my throat. "I'll kill you first."

She shrugged, her dress rustling. "Doubtful. Tell me what you know of the prophecy."

"The what?"

"Nothing?" Her nose wrinkled in disgust. "All this to capture you, and you know nothing? What a disappointment you are."

"Anything that pisses you off makes me happy," I gasped out, trying to kick the damned rats so I could free myself.

"Oh, I almost forgot. I expressly forbid you from hurting me."

*Fuck!*

"And you will *never* be queen, so abandon that delusion." Her face soured with something like jealousy.

"Where are you getting this from?" I laughed, sneering like I wasn't terrified for myself and everyone I loved.

"You've been strangely well behaved," she remarked, the jealousy wiped away in a heartbeat as she patted my cheek and stepped back. "So I'll answer your question. There was a Greenheart crone, twenty years ago, who foretold your marriage and your failed assassination of the prince."

I scowled. She didn't have to remind me of my failure. I *hated* failing at shit, even if I was glad Kier was still alive. I speared my soul towards him again, desperate to reach him. There was a gaping chasm between us, full of empty darkness.

Any hope I had of getting out of this alive splintered.

"She said you will become the Bluescale Queen, with Kier at your side, a force so powerful than no one will stand against you."

I blinked. Nice. Queen suited me. I could just imagine the heft of a crown on my head.

It was insane of course; seers and psychics didn't exist outside of stories.

"The current king is lazy and careless, but with Kier and *you* in power?" Cleordora's expression twisted as she turned away, stalking a few paces before pinning me with a look that should have killed me where I stood. "You're a threat I can't abide. You'll come for my kingdom."

"So you're getting in first?" I asked bitterly, a laugh

stuck in my throat. "Conquer us before we can conquer you?"

"Exactly that," she agreed, and gestured at her rats.

They rushed from my legs with scratches and bites, their furry bodies sliding against me and making my skin crawl. The moment I could move, I leapt out of their huddle and patted my legs, making sure there were none left on me. They might have been harmless babies, but with their master they were bone-chilling, and I couldn't stop shaking.

"What makes you think we even want your shitty little kingdom?" I asked while I panted, gathering my composure.

The second I could breathe again, I flexed my hands, watched the blue magic flash in response to my call, and I threw a sapphire blaze through the air with as much power and rage as I could call up. I was *furious,* so I had a lot of rage to fuel my blow.

I had a moment of satisfaction, watching my magic sharpen into twin swords and drive all the way through Cleodora's chest, one in each tit. She growled, low in her throat; her claws erupted with green magic as she slashed an answering blow at me.

Before her claws could even hit me, pain arrowed through my chest and I crashed to my knees in the grass with a guttural scream. It came from deep in my soul, bruising its way through my chest. Pain blistered across my skin, tore into my insides, and sank into my core of power. My magic cut out abruptly, my rings dull.

"I warned you," she panted, "not to hurt me, or you'd regret it. Now your own body is your worst enemy."

I curled over my knees, clenching my teeth against

more screams, refusing to give her the sick satisfaction. *Bitch. Raging, heartless, power-mad bitch.*

I jerked when she patted my head. "Good puppet. Now run back to your dear husband, and know the consequences should you try to hurt me or breathe a word of what happened here."

The blood drained from my face. "I can't go back."

Not while she lived in my head, not while she *controlled* me.

"You have no choice," she replied, a smile warming her face, making her even more beautiful. It was poison, that beauty. I choked on it, and bit back pain as it splintered through all the vital places inside me.

"Kier will feel it. He'll feel the pain and know something is wrong."

Cleodora laughed softly. "With the wave of magic blocking you off from him? He hasn't felt a thing. And you know what will happen if you so much as hint at it."

I panted, my nostrils flaring, and hissed when her fingers dug into my chin, tipping my face up to meet hers.

"I own you, Zaba."

"I'll destroy you for this," I rasped, wrenching my face out of her hold and staggering to my feet.

My whole body shook, pain echoing through my soul like shockwaves of torture. I couldn't feel her in my mind, couldn't even sense the hooks of her command in me. If she was in my head, she was everywhere, untraceable.

Would I ever get her out?

I knew the answer to that, but I didn't want to admit it.

"Return to your husband," she ordered casually, straightening her crown on her head. "Kiss him, tell him you were hurt and scared, but that everything is okay now."

"Fuck you," I spat, lifting my foot to kick her between the legs, but walking instead—away from her.

*No!*

I snarled, fighting my foot as it lifted in another step, then another. Nothing stopped my legs from walking, not even the deadly wave of magic that arched over me, crackling and hot, making humans and goblins alike scream on the other side.

The wall fell when I was within one foot of it, vanishing like it had never been there. Cleodora laughed softly when I flinched.

"Better run, Zaba. Kier will be missing you."

I turned, my teeth bared in a goblin gesture I'd learned from Aerona, but the queen was gone. Screams died across the field, turning to pained moans and cries of grief.

My foot took another step, then another. My ears rang with the sudden drop in air pressure, the absence of the queen's oppressive magic making my head spun.

What just happened...? But I knew. I couldn't escape or deny it. My legs took another three steps, carrying me into slaughter and carnage.

I reeled, my breaths coming in pants.

The greenheart queen had made me a spy in my own kingdom. Anything Kier shared with me, I'd be forced to tell her.

"Well, fuck you, Cleodora," I snarled, and turned the other way, walking—into a brick wall. At least that was what it felt like; I slammed into solid air and couldn't take another step.

*Please.*

A growl of rage shook my throat. A vein felt like it burst in my eye as I screamed and fought against the magic holding me back. No, the *compulsion* holding me back. Every part of my body demanded that I turn and find Kier; I couldn't fight it.

My legs carried me across the field, past bloodied corpses and goblin bodies. But the sounds of rage and grief were muted, the world strangely muffled as I walked, unerringly, to Kier.

What was the point in fighting? *I own you, Zaba.*

Kier was surrounded by an aura of blue magic, not quite the vivid glow of other goblins, more like a dark blue cloud. As if the Haar and his magic had fused.

*"Zaba!"* he roared when he spotted me. He stormed across the field like a wrathful god, not paying attention to anyone or anything around him.

I walked numbly, my heart hollowed out and my hands still shaking. I opened my mouth to warn him to stay away, that I wasn't safe, but—

*Run back to your dear husband, and know the consequences should you try to hurt me or breathe a word of what happened here.*

I flinched away from the thought, my mind lingering on the sight of Natasya murdered and Zaugustus burned to a blackened husk. Not Kier, too. I couldn't lose him, too.

But spying on him? Betraying him? Again?

He'd never forgive me. He'd hate me for eternity.

I felt sick when he finally reached me, and I knew he could read it in my expression, but I couldn't hide it.

"It's okay," he breathed, gathering me close. The heat and strength of him bled into my frozen body and made my knees buckle. A sob emerged as a small, broken noise. "You're okay. I've got you."

I shook in his arms, air reaching my lungs in broken

gasps. I had no control over my head as it tilted, my lips pressing to Kier's throat. *Kiss him.*

I sobbed harder, shaking so hard my bones and teeth rattled.

"Zaba?" he asked, concern wrapping like warmth around the numbness in my soul.

"I got hurt, my—my side, someone stabbed me."

My voice but not my words.

*Tell him you were hurt.*

"Fuck," he growled, wrenching back to inspect my wound. It was still weeping blood, but I was numb to it all, my fingers locked around the hem of his shirt. I didn't know where his coat had gone, but his shirt was soaked in sweat and splattered with blood.

I tried to speak my own words—Kier, please, you have to run, you have to run from me—and nothing emerged.

I could hardly stand to look at him.

"I was—I was scared," I rasped, struggling to breathe, his scent filling my senses and making me sick at the betrayal.

*And scared.*

"No one will ever hurt you again," Kier snarled fiercely, his eyes flashing with violent protectiveness. "I *swear,* Zaba. Tell me who hurt you and I'll burn the heart out of each and every one of them."

My tears flowed freely, hot and ashamed. "Everything is okay now."

*But that everything is okay now.*

Except the Greenheart Queen had me under her control.

Except I'd lost control of my mind, body, and my soul.

Except I would betray him.

And this time, it would break us both in ways we could never heal from.

Kier folded me back into his arms, choking me on the scent of pine, blood, and magic. It smelled like home, safety, and *love*—all the things I needed so badly I couldn't stop shaking. Everything I was compelled to burn to ashes.

"Everything is okay," Kier agreed, kissing my temple and oblivious to the snake in his den.

THANK you so much for reading Letta and Kier's second book. We hope you loved it as much as the Goblin's Bride, and thank you so much for supporting the series by picking up this book. It so very nearly didn't happen because the series didn't find many readers, and it would've been heartbreaking to leave Kier and Letta apart. You can never know how much it means that you love this story.

More is to come from these two, with the final book The Wicked Queen, which will be available to preorder soon!

THE BEST WAY TO stay up to date with releases is to follow us on Amazon, or join our newsletters, which you can do by grabbing **a free Kier POV of the wedding in book one.** Bonus: you can learn just how grumpy and broody Kier really is.

We'll see you again in book three—if you want the book ASAP let us know, and share the series with your reader friends. The more demand, the sooner we can write it.

THANKS AGAIN,
    Leigh & Lysandra
    xx

# KIER'S POV OF THE WEDDING SCENE!

If you ever wondered what Kier was thinking when he married his human enemy, now you can find out!

JOIN MY MAILING LIST FOR YOUR FREE STORY

## BOOK THREE: THE WICKED QUEEN

Return to Letta and Kier's world of magic, enemies, and intrigue in the third and final A Feud So Dark and Lovely book.

PREORDER IT NOW

## COMPLETE RH ANGEL/DEMON FANTASY SERIES!

Betrayed by heaven, protected by hell. The devil and his hellhounds will do anything to keep their angel safe.

READ FREE IN KINDLE UNLIMITED

# SIGNED LEIGH KELSEY BOOKS!

https://payhip.com/snarkystabbybooks

You can find all my available print copies in my online book store, plus books from my cowrites and pen-names, **and all signed orders come with swag and a dedication from yours truly.**

VISIT THE STORE: https://payhip.com/ snarkystabbybooks

# ABOUT LEIGH KELSEY

Leigh Kelsey writes about psychos with questionable morals and addictions to shiny, stabby objects, but she's perfectly harmless, she swears. She can be found in Yorkshire, England listening to K-Pop, watching serial killer documentaries, and writing as much spicy paranormal romance as she possibly can in a day.

LEIGH KELSEY

WHERE THE MEN ARE *PSYCHO* BUT THE WOMEN ARE *WICKED*

# FIND THESE OTHER BOOKS BY LEIGH KELSEY!

Feared by Monsters: A stand-alone twisted paranormal romance

*Sick and Twisted series*

*(Twisted Death Gods RH)*

All Hallows Night

All Hallows Game

All Hallows Trick

All Hallows Masque

*Kissed By Brimstone series*

*(Twisted Paranormal Demon RH)*

Hellborn Angel

Midnight Descent

Eternal Night

Cursed Dawn

Shadow Fall: Part 1

Shadow Fall: Part 2

*A Feud So Dark And Lovely series*

*(Enemies To Lovers MF Romance)*

The Goblin's Bride

The Doomed Prince

The Wicked Queen (Winter 2025)

*Fae of the Saintlands series*

*(Enemies To Lovers RH Romance)*

Books 1-3 Box Set

Heir of Ruin

Heart of Thorns

Kiss of Iron

Touch of Darkness

Court of Wolves

*Shadowfire Mates/Blacktower Prison series*

*(Complete Dragon Shifter Romance series)*

Complete Series Box Set

Start with Prison of Embers

*Lili Kazana series*

*(Complete RH Angel/Demon Romance series)*

Complete Series Box Set

Start with Cast From Heaven

# ABOUT LYSANDRA GLASS

Lysandra Glass is a fantasy romance author from the UK. After falling in love with too many dark, brooding fictional men, she now writes her own stories full of forbidden romance, enemies who fall in love, and vast fantasy worlds teeming with goblins, fae, and elves. Her debut book, The Goblin's Bride, is out now!

# FIND THESE OTHER BOOKS BY LYSANDRA GLASS!

All books free on Kindle Unlimited

*A Feud So Dark And Lovely series*
*(Enemies To Lovers MF Romance)*
The Goblin's Bride
The Doomed Prince
The Wicked Queen (Winter 2025)

*Villain Gets The Girl Stand-Alone*
Stalking Wendy Darling

*Heir of Wyvara series*
*(Fae Arranged Marriage MF Romance)*
Wings of Cruelty and Flame